T

Kingsley Edge, The 8th Circle's King of Kink, has instructed his top dominatrix to write down some "best practices" that he can share with the club's other professional dominants.

Mistress Nora—who also moonlights as an erotic romance writer—turns his request into a series of sexy shorts For His Eyes Only.

The Mistress Files collects five of Mistress Nora's favorite client stories from Kingsley's files, from a rock star with a secret to a male "switch" with an itch for more than just pain.

THE ORIGINAL SINNERS PULP LIBRARY

Vintage paperback-inspired editions of standalone novels and novellas from *USA Today* bestseller Tiffany Reisz's million-copy selling Original Sinners erotic romance series. Learn more at tiffanyreisz.com.

THE ORIGINAL SINNERS
PULP LIBRARY

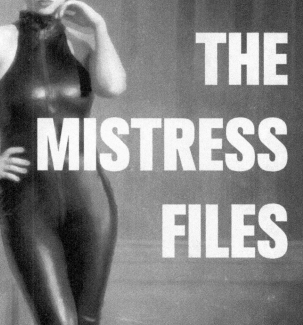

THE
MISTRESS
FILES

THE MISTRESS FILES

TIFFANY REISZ

8TH CIRCLE PRESS · LOUISVILLE, KY

THE MISTRESS FILES copyright © 2013 Tiffany Reisz

All rights reserved. No part of this publications may be reproduced, stored in a retrieval system, or transmitted, in any form or by any means, electronic, mechanical, photocopying, recording, or otherwise, without the prior written permission of the publisher, 8th Circle Press, a division of 8th Circle, Louisville, Kentucky, U.S.A.

All characters appearing in this work are fictitious. Any resemblance to real persons, living, or dead, is purely coincidental.

Previously published by Harlequin Books/Mills & Boon as *The Mistress Files: An Original Sinners Novella*

Cover design by Andrew Shaffer

Front cover image contains a photo used under license from iStock by Getty Images. Interior images public domain.

Mass-Market Paperback ISBN: 978-1-949769-20-3

Also available as an ebook

First 8th Circle Press edition March 2021

Second Edition

I'm writing this for one reason and one reason only—Kingsley is paying me to do it. Well, that and he ordered me to do it. And he's gorgeous and I have trouble telling him "no" when he pouts. Okay, maybe I have more than one reason for doing it.

But I still don't want to do it.

Kingsley, do you have any idea what a huge and obnoxious undertaking this is? Writing client profiles? Do you know how many clients I have? And no, I'm not going to talk to you as long as you're reading over my shoulder while I type.

Since you're reading over my shoulder, I'm going to insult you every chance I get. I know you want me to write these files "so zee other dominants can learn from me how to better treat zee clients." And yes, you do sound like that,

Frenchy. Now stop breathing in my ear and let me write.

I'm going to use real names here—you can have Juliette change them later.

Oh, and I'm doing the Sir Arthur Conan Doyle-esque titles on purpose, and if you change them I'll set your bed on fire. And NOT in a good way this time.

— "Mistress Nora" Sutherlin
New York City

CONTENTS

FILE #1

Client Name: Sheridan Stratford (age 23)

Profession: Actress, currently starring in *Empire City* as the virginal daughter of a corrupt billionaire CEO. She's known colloquially in the press as "America's Sweetheart" because of her slight stature, her innocent youthful looks and natural blond hair.

Inclination: Submissive

Level of Experience: None

Orientation: Straight but flexible

* * *

Sheridan's not attracted to women, but when she came to me she had a problem she didn't trust a man to solve. Probably because a man caused it. I'm a woman. Hard to hide that fact (D-cups, thank you very much, Mother Nature), but I'm a damn fine cross-dresser and only Kingsley looks better in a three-piece suit than I do. The man annoys the piss out of me on an almost daily basis, but I'll be the first to admit, the frog is a prince.

And an ass at times who should treat his best dominatrix better and give her chocolate and martinis on a daily basis.

(I know you're still reading over my shoulder, Kingsley. Go away. Don't you have your secretary to violate or something?)

But back to the point. Sheridan. Ah…Sheridan. Dominants take note—it's a terrible idea to fall for your clients. Terrible. Verboten. Don't even think of doing it.

Unless you're me. I did it. But only a little. You wouldn't blame me if you could see this girl. Oh, wait. She's on TV. You have seen her so you understand. Beautiful little waif—in her early twenties, she hardly looks a day over eighteen. So petite and fragile, she's like a glass flower you want to hold in your palm and marvel at the intricacy of each flowing line until your close your hand around it and crush it into a thousand pieces.

I'm sorry. I might have just had an orgasm.

Back to Sheridan. Love this girl. How could I

not? She was practically trembling the first time I saw her in person on the roof of Kingsley's townhouse holding a candlestick in the conservatory...

You know, I think I'm getting my job mixed up with *Clue* again. Come to think of it, *Clue* would have been a much darker, more interesting game had it been about a sex crime instead of a murder.

Digression over. I'm sorry. I get verbose in first person, which is why I should never write it in. Let's fix that, shall we?

Dear Reader, just imagine Sheridan Stratford—an ingénue of Broadway, the sweet starlet of the small screen—sitting on an antique fainting couch in a moonlit conservatory on the roof of a Manhattan townhouse. Silver slip dress, strappy heels on stick-thin ankles, long pale hair in a loose knot, eyes wide and scared.

Scared but brave.

That's my girl.

THE CASE OF THE ACTING
ACTRESS

Sheridan whispered something into her glass of wine and what she whispered The Mistress would never know. "Help me," perhaps. "What am I doing here," maybe. Sheridan took a sip and then another before setting the glass down on the table next to the vase of white orchids. The Mistress merely waited in the shadows of the doorway and watched her for a moment, trying to read the girl's body language. Shoulders slumped, head down, feet that never stopped moving even though she remained seated. The Mistress could glean two facts from the moves Sheridan made—one fact true and one fact terrible. The girl was terrified. True. And the girl was ashamed.

Terrible.

From Kingsley, The Mistress had learned why Sheridan had come to them. But her reasons didn't really matter. The clients came from everywhere. They were everyone. And every last one of them told them a different reason for coming to The Underground.

My wife won't tie me up…

My boyfriend can't touch me right…

My mother said I was sick…

I have these dreams every night that won't stop…

I need to be hurt or I can't come…

I need to be punished to feel loved…

A thousand reasons that could all be boiled down, stripped bare, and divided into one of two real reasons…

I'm here because I want this.

I'm here because I need this.

The Mistress wasn't a prostitute, though she respected their work. As a dominatrix, she never let a client touch her, never let a client inside her. Never inside her *body*, anyway. Sometimes on rare occasions, if the client was particularly beautiful or especially broken, The Mistress let the client inside her heart.

Sheridan had wealth from her acting career, and wealth meant power. But it was a powerless little girl who sat under the glass roof that night. And when a tender leaf on one of the orchids dropped off the plant and landed on the floor, Sheridan stood up and walked quickly to the sink by the cutting station and dumped out her glass of wine before refilling it with cold water and pouring it into the plant.

The Mistress smiled to herself as Sheridan turned wine into water so she could give a little drink to a thirsty flower she'd never met before. And that's when Sheridan first crawled inside The Mistress's heart.

Digging into her pocket, The Mistress found her silver lighter and brought a cigarette to her lips. She flicked on the flame with a quick, loud snap. Sheridan gasped at the sudden noise and spun around so fast she dropped her empty wine glass onto the floor, shattering it into a thousand glinting shards.

"Oh, God. I'm so sorry," Sheridan said, raising a hand to her flushed forehead. She stared down at the glass on the floor, her face a mask of utter shock and self-loathing. It broke The Mistress's heart to see such an ugly look on that beautiful face. Then and there, she resolved to wipe the shame off that face for all eternity.

The Mistress made no move. Whatever happened, no matter how emotional the client got, The Mistress had long ago learned that she must remain calm in every situation. Even when screaming German curses while beating a client with a birch rod, she must be calm inside, at peace, and always in control. The clients didn't just pay for that, they deserved it.

As Sheridan looked down in horror at the broken glass, The Mistress merely brought the lighter to the tip of the cigarette, and lit it as she stepped forward out of the shadows.

"Leave it," The Mistress ordered. "Just a wine glass. Kingsley has millions of them."

"I'll pay for it, Ma'am. I promise."

"You'll do no such thing. I'll make him pay you for daring to give you a glass that breakable. Now go. Sit over there and forget about the glass."

The Mistress nodded toward a settee at the edge of the conservatory. From there, one could look out and see a thousand windows lit from within by artificial lights and shining from without by the Manhattan moonlight.

Sheridan rushed to obey, nearly skidding on the slick floor in the process. She sat on the silk cushions and crossed her legs. Such a little slip of a thing... The Mistress wanted to gather her close and hold her until she stopped being so scared of herself. But The Mistress didn't touch her, merely sat down next to her and took a long draw on her cigarette before blowing the smoke out.

"I don't smoke," The Mistress said as the last of the white cloud reached the glass roof.

"But..." Sheridan squeaked one word out before falling silent again.

"But I'm smoking? Well, yeah, you got me there. I have this client. Some music publishing company bajillionaire. Total masochist. He's a human ashtray. All I have to do is use him as a footstool, smoke a cigarette, and then put it out on his naked back. He orgasms so hard that Niagara Falls says, 'Damn. Someone get the mop there.' Easy job. Fifteen-minute session. I charge him five-thousand dollars for it. Plus twelve dollars for the plastic drop-cloth."

Sheridan blanched. Apparently the thought of putting a cigarette out on someone's bare back didn't sound like an "easy job" to her. But then again, that's why The Mistress made that kind of money. She walked a fine line with every client—a line of morality, legality, sexuality. Any one of her clients could take their injuries, bought and paid for, to the police and report an assault. The Mistress took a risk with every client. The bigger the risk, the bigger the payday.

She did love her paydays.

The Mistress took one last draw on her cigarette before stubbing it out in the soil of the nearest plant. Sheridan's eyes widened even more, and The Mistress had to use all her willpower not to kiss the poor thing.

"I like pissing off Kingsley. You can tell him I did that."

Sheridan laughed nervously. "I wouldn't do that. He terrifies me."

"Sheridan, I have a feeling everything terrifies you."

Wincing, the girl nodded.

"Look." The Mistress held out her empty hands and tugged melodramatically at her cuffs. "Nothing up my sleeves. No crops. No canes. No floggers. No knives, whips, or guns. Nothing to be afraid of here. No one's going to hurt you."

"But…isn't that what you do?"

"Yes, if that's what my client wants. Not all my clients are masochists. I've got medical fetishists, foot fetishists…I have a college professor who likes to drink human urine. I've got a world-famous surgeon who's into cross-dressing and Domestic discipline. I bring him my laundry and order him to iron it while he's naked but for an apron. I only hurt the ones who want to be hurt. And obviously tonight you don't want to be hurt. The question is…what do you want?"

"I'm sorry. I don't even know why I'm here. This is ridiculous. You're not going to be able to help me, and I'm wasting your time—"

"Slow down there, beautiful. We just got started. First of all, tell me what your problem is, and then we'll figure out if I can help you or not."

"Didn't Kingsley tell you?"

"He told me. I want to hear it from you."

Sheridan paused and took a deep breath. She tugged at the hem of her dress. Her right foot worried the floor with tapping. "I can't…" She took another deeper breath. "I can't orgasm anymore."

"Nonsense. You just *don't* orgasm. You still can."

"I haven't. Not for years. I try. I had a couple boyfriends. Gorgeous boyfriends. Smart, sexy, sweet. Really nice guys. And they tried everything. Not since Rex..." There she stopped and dropped her head again in shame.

"This was the man you lost your virginity to?"

Sheridan nodded.

"You were pretty young the first time?"

She sighed. "Yeah. I know—"

"Did you tell him no?"

"No. I told him 'yes.' He asked, and I said 'yes.' I had a huge crush on him. I didn't want to tell him 'no.' I loved it."

The girl said "loved" with vehemence and passion, and for the first time since meeting her, The Mistress felt like she had could see the real Sheridan lurking under all that fear and shame.

"You know our Kingsley lost his virginity at thirteen—tops. Older girl. That wicked Frenchman was a lady-killer from birth. He tells the story of his first time and he gets congratulated like he won the fucking lottery. Double-standards can suck my cock. Don't be ashamed that you liked it. You didn't do anything wrong by saying 'yes,' and you didn't do anything wrong by liking it. Excuse me, by loving it. The fault is on Rex. Not you. He'll answer to God for it. You can answer to me."

At that Sheridan burst into laughter—real laughter, not the nervous kind. "Thank you. I needed that."

"You're welcome. I don't have a cock, by the way. Not a real one. I have a pretty impressive assortment of the artificial variety back at the club. I thought for our first session we'd stick to the basics."

"The basics?"

The Mistress held up both hands and wiggled her fingers.

Sheridan blushed. "The basics. I get it."

"Good girl. Now you say the guys you've been with since Rex tried everything. I assume you mean oral sex, digital stimulation, vaginal intercourse…"

Sheridan nodded, her face still a becoming shade of pale red.

"Did they try vibrators?"

"One did. But I couldn't relax enough."

"Can you have them on your own?"

"Sometimes, but only if I'm fantasizing about Rex and stuff we did. It's just…depressing. I don't even miss him. I just miss…it. Whatever it was."

The Mistress sat back, threw her legs onto the settee and crossed her feet, clad in black and white Oxfords, at the ankles. "I'm depressed just hearing about it. We've got to get your pussy back in business. Take your clothes off."

Sheridan froze.

The Mistress grinned. "I love that reaction. The now-the-shit-gets-real reaction. I think it's my favorite part of the job. That and the money. And the clothes. And all the rich and famous people who are afraid of me because I know their kinks. Okay, I have a lot of favorite parts of this job. Anyway, I just noticed that you still have your clothes on, and I'm fairly certain I gave you an order." The Mistress paused and tapped her temple. "Yes, I've reviewed the tapes. It was an order."

Still Sheridan didn't move to obey.

The Mistress narrowed her eyes at the girl. "What did you like so much about what Rex did to you?" she asked. "Tell me in one sentence."

"He…" Sheridan began. "He was older and in charge and made me feel like I was the center of the universe."

"Look up." The Mistress pointed at the roof and Sheridan turned to look at the glass. "The night is watching us. Sheridan. You are the center of the universe. And if the center of the universe doesn't take her clothes off in the next ten seconds, the center of the universe is going to get turned over my knee and spanked like the stubborn, recalcitrant child she is."

That did it. Sheridan stood up and unzipped

the back of her dress and shimmied out it. It landed like a pool of quicksilver at her feet. She had come prepared, The Mistress noted with pleasure—no panties on and no bra. Only her strappy shoes remained on her feet. She bent to remove them.

"No. Leave the shoes on. Stand there for one hot minute. I'm taking a mental picture."

Sheridan froze in a perfect pose of modest beauty. With her head turned slightly to the side and her hands lightly clasped in front of her and her face a mask of elegant composure, the thin girl with small breasts transformed into an ancient Greek statue of Aphrodite turned to flesh. The Mistress smiled at her statue. All she'd had to do was order the girl to pose for a photograph, and Sheridan turned into the professional actress who commanded six figures an episode.

"You're stunning. You know that, don't you?" The Mistress asked.

Sheridan shrugged her shoulders.

"I suppose you hear it all the time from fans and casting agents," The Mistress said. "But I'm not a fan. I'm not a director. I don't have to suck up to you to get you to spread for me. You're paying me for the privilege of spreading for me. You paid up front. I have no reason to lie. Say, 'Thank you for telling me I'm stunning, Mistress.'"

"Thank you for telling me I'm stunning, Mistress."

"Good. There's hope for you yet. Now sit." The Mistress moved her legs from the settee to the floor and pointed to the crimson cushions. Sheridan sat back down as she kept her legs tightly pressed together. "Stay there."

The Mistress pulled off her necktie and un-knotted it. "I'm going to blindfold you. It'll help you relax and focus on what you're feeling. Do you have a safe word?"

"Kingsley told me I should pick one. It's Mc-Carthy's."

"Like the single malt whiskey?"

Sheridan smiled. "You know your alcohol."

"Of course I do. I'm Catholic. You like whiskey?"

"Hate it. But Rex liked it. Straight."

"He sounds Catholic."

The smile on Sheridan's face broadened and The Mistress nearly blinked at the brightness. The Mistress could only imagine how this girl could light up a stage.

"I can still remember what his mouth tasted like. I never wanted to drink the stuff. I was happy tasting it on him."

"McCarthy's it is then. I want you to be able to tell me yes, no, stop, go while we're playing. You'll say McCarthy's if and only if you want to stop completely, take off the blindfold, and end the scene. I'll be touching your body, and every woman is different. You can give me directions. If I'm doing something that doesn't work for you, tell me. You can give me encouragement if I'm doing something that does. Understand?"

"I understand."

The Mistress glared at the girl so hard she winced.

"I mean, yes, Mistress."

"Better. Hold still." Careful of Sheridan's perfectly coiffed hair, The Mistress brought the tie over her head, placed it on Sheridan's blinking eyes, and knotted it at the nape of her neck. "Too tight?"

"No…it's fine. Thank you, Mistress."

"You're welcome."

"I didn't expect…" Sheridan began and paused.

"What didn't you expect?"

"I didn't think you'd be nice. I don't think 'nice' when I hear the word 'dominatrix.'"

"I'm nice to all my clients even when I'm beating the shit out of them. 'Nice' means treating someone how they want to be treated. Tonight you want to be treated with gentleness. Next time maybe you want to be treated with pain. Sounds nice, right?"

Sheridan smiled. "I might not say no."

"Good. Now lie down on your back and breathe. Breathe slowly and deeply. I'm going to put my hands on your legs, but that's it. I won't touch any other part of you without warning you first."

Sheridan obeyed but not without tentativeness. Every line of her body vibrated with fear as she rolled onto her back and slowly stretched out her legs. The Mistress decided to let the fear work in her favor. Adrenaline rushes made for beautiful orgasms. Adrenaline…

"Sheridan…" The Mistress placed her hands on Sheridan's thighs right above her knees. "Were you scared when you were with Rex?"

"No. Yes." She laughed as The Mistress began to rub her thighs. "Scared isn't the right word. But he was older than me. I was…intimidated, maybe. Rex was definitely intimidating. Strong, silent type. Sexy. Smart. I could never quite believe it was happening even when he was inside me."

"With your most recent boyfriend, did you ever feel scared or intimidated?"

Sheridan shook her head as The Mistress made slow, easy strokes with her hand up and down the girl's thin legs. "Not a bit. Brett was so nice, goofy, very sweet guy. Like a big kid."

"And you let him fuck you?" The Mistress asked with mock horror.

"I feel like I should apologize to you, Mistress."

"No. No need," she sighed. "The damage is

already done. No wonder you couldn't orgasm. Must have been like letting your brother try to fuck you. No sexual tension equals no orgasm, especially for a woman like you."

"A woman like me? What am I?"

"You're a sub. No doubt in my mind."

The Mistress continued to caress Sheridan's bare legs. The girl wasn't more than five feet tall, but half of that was leg.

"Like a submissive?" Sheridan asked.

"Exactly like that. You need to be dominated to feel sexual, yes? Intimidated? Overpowered? Maybe even a little scared?"

"Yes. Definitely. That's exactly it. Nothing Brett did made me feel anything. I thought I loved him because I liked him so much."

"Liking can get in the way of lusting a lot of the times. Some of my best orgasms have come from men I wanted to beat into unconsciousness. You know, after they were done fucking me."

"It would be nice to be with someone who makes me feel like it's, I don't know…"

"Like it's an honor to be with him? Like you're his personal sexual property? Like you exist just to spread your legs for him whenever he orders you to?"

"That, Mistress."

"I know the feeling. Trust me."

"I kind of…I sort of feel that with you. Kingsley said you weren't taking any new clients.

Too busy. Too in demand. But you made an exception for me."

"Of course I did. I saw you."

Sheridan blushed. The Mistress slid her hands between Sheridan's thighs and gently pressed them apart. They opened easily for her. Good. Tension helped with an orgasm. Terror didn't.

"I've topped royalty," The Mistress said, wanting to remind her new client just how lucky she was to be in her capable hands. "Real royalty with bodyguards standing right outside the door the entire time. Rock stars. Politicians. Millionaires. Billionaires. I could name them and you'd faint from shock that they were in the scene. That's how important I am. That's how busy I am. But Kingsley told me about you. I watched an interview you did. The reporter asked you if you had a boyfriend. I've never seen a sadder, faker smile in my life, Little Miss."

"I like that," Sheridan confessed as The Mistress caressed the sensitive skin of her inner thighs.

"Like that I've topped rich and famous people? Richer and more famous than you? Or liked that I watched your interview?"

Sheridan shook her head. "I liked that you called me Little Miss."

Once again, The Mistress was seized with a

nearly unconquerable urge to kiss the girl. But she restrained herself. Just barely.

"Glad you like it. That's what I'll call you from now on—my Little Miss. Now, my Little Miss needs to take a deep breath. I'm going to start touching more of you—arms, stomach, hips, and breasts in that order."

"Yes, Mistress." Sheridan nodded her nervous little head and The Mistress moved in closer between Sheridan's open thighs.

As promised, she started with Sheridan's arms at the wrists and stroked upwards to her shoulders with dancing fingertips. Delicate shivers passed through Sheridan's body at the lightness of the touch.

The Mistress trailed her fingers down Sheridan's arms to her wrists again, before crossing over to the girl's trembling stomach. The Mistress laid her hand flat under her ribcage and felt the muscles flutter underneath.

She tickled Sheridan's narrow girlish hips with her thumbs, tracing the bones. "You need to eat more, Little Miss."

"I eat all the time, Mistress. I promise. I just can't gain weight. I'm going to look fourteen forever."

"There are worse fates—working for Kingsley, for starters."

Sheridan gave a little giggle. "I like him. Is he really that bad?"

"Terrible. It's impossible to get any work done with him around talking French at you and being all suave and seductive. Sometimes I fuck him just to shut him up."

"Poor you, Mistress."

"Tell me about it."

As Sheridan dissolved again into laughter, The Mistress slid her hands upwards and covered the girl's breasts with both hands.

Then the laughter stopped.

The Mistress smiled. Just the reaction she wanted.

At first, The Mistress did nothing but let the heat of her hands seep into Sheridan's body through her breasts. Under her palms, she felt Sheridan's nipples harden.

"You have beautiful breasts, Little Miss. Perfectly shaped. Beautiful nipples the color of pink roses."

"I have no breasts. I'm an A-cup." Sheridan sounded genuinely upset with her own body. "I should get implants. My agent says—"

"Fuck your agent. You get implants and you could lose sensitivity. Are fake boobs really worth never feeling this again?" The Mistress punctuated her sentence by gently pinching both of Sheridan's nipples, a move that elicited one of the more erotic gasps ever uttered since the invention of gasping.

"No...I'd hate to lose that," Sheridan confessed.

"Then don't. Your body is perfect. Don't fuck with it. That's my job."

"Yes, Mistress."

"Good girl. Now shut up and lay there. I've got a girl to get off."

A new smile appeared on Sheridan's face in place of the old, nervous smile. This smile was amorous, heated, sexy beyond description and exactly what The Mistress was going for.

For a good ten minutes (a very good ten minutes in The Mistress's estimation) she focused her attentions on Sheridan's breasts, nipples, and chest. Men rarely understood the power of focusing attention on one part of the body at a time. A few lucky women could even achieve orgasm from breast stimulation alone. The Mistress doubted Sheridan had that power, but she'd need as much foreplay as she could stand if the long-awaited orgasm was to come.

The Mistress moved slowly...tracing circles around Sheridan's breast with a fingertip before spiraling up to her nipple and back down again. Pinches turned to gentle kneading. Soon Sheridan's chest moved in rapid pants and her nipples turned from pale pink to red.

"Are you enjoying this, Little Miss?"

"So much...you really know what you're doing."

"I've got a gift for giving women orgasms. I give myself an orgasm at least once a day."

Sheridan giggled again and her blush deepened. Good. Flushed skin was one of the tell-tale signs of an aroused woman. But it would take more than just stimulating her body to get Sheridan to orgasm. The Mistress needed to get inside her mind.

"You know, Little Miss, this isn't my only job," The Mistress said as she ran her fingers over Sheridan's collarbone, giving her breasts a moment to recover from all the attention. "I'm also a writer."

"Really?"

"I write erotica. I love a good sexy story. Reading them, writing them, hearing them."

"Me too. I learned all about sex from my mother's romance novels. I think that's why when Rex came onto me that first time, I jumped at the chance. I couldn't wait to try out all this stuff I'd been reading about."

"How did the reality of sex compare to the fictional version?"

Sheridan sighed. "It was definitely different. I was in my dad's office for one thing. In the books, they're always in a bed...or maybe a carriage. Not bent over an armchair or flat on a desk."

"Never fucked in a carriage. I'll have to put that on my bucket list. Continue."

"It hurt more than I expected. In the books, there's always just this quick stab of pain and then ecstasy."

"Well, it's the writer's way of throwing in some drama to an otherwise simple and natural act. But too much pain and drama, and it turns into a horror story."

Sheridan grinned and lifted her hips. Another good sign. Sheridan couldn't seem to stop moving her lower body. That meant she was feeling something in the right spot.

"It wasn't a horror story. Definitely. It just really burned going in. I was wet and excited but not ready. Not really. The next time was a lot better."

"Can you remember your favorite time with him? The best sex? The best orgasm?"

"Yes. Like it was yesterday."

"Tell me about it. I'm going to start touching your clit, by the way, while you tell me about the best sex you ever had. Don't argue with me about it."

"I wouldn't." She shook her head and took a quick, deep breath. "I was eighteen...about to leave Chicago and move to New York. I'd done some commercials and got an agent. My dreams were coming true. But..."

"But you had to leave Rex behind."

"Right. I didn't want him to know I was going. If he tried to talk me out of it, he might have. So I knew it would be our last time for a few months at least. I went to his house one evening. He wasn't expecting me. My flight left the very next morning, but I didn't tell him that."

"What did he do?"

"He opened the door and saw me standing on the stoop. He pulled me inside, and without saying anything he kissed me."

"Very nice."

"I loved when he did that. Every time I showed up on his doorstep, I was afraid I'd make him mad. Maybe he'd have company over or something and wish I hadn't shown up. I wasn't even his mistress. I was just his dirty secret. But every time I went over there...yeah, just like that."

"And then?"

"And then he was all over me...right in the foyer. I had on a plaid skirt—"

"How very Catholic schoolgirl of you."

"Episcopal, actually."

"Don't kill my lady-boner. I'm pretending it was Catholic. Go on. He was all over you how?"

"Hands everywhere. Mouth everywhere. He liked to bite when he kissed me. My lips and tongue and neck and ears. He'd dig under my skirt and shove his hand into my panties."

"You wore panties around him? Such a waste of time."

"Only because I loved hearing him grunt with frustration when he had to drag them off of me."

"I like your style. And I'm about to touch your clit and vagina. Continue."

Sheridan stiffened but kept talking. "So yes... plaid skirt," she said and inhaled right as The Mistress put her fingertip gently to her clitoris. Her whole body tensed, but The Mistress did nothing and said nothing, merely waited. Sheridan continued. "And there was this table in the foyer—fancy table. His housekeeper always kept fresh flowers on it."

"How nice." The Mistress gently kneaded Sheridan's clitoris with one finger. The attentions The Mistress had paid to Sheridan's breasts had sent the blood flowing in the right direction. Sheridan's labia had started to open and her clitoris had swollen slightly.

"Those poor flowers never knew what hit them. Everything on that table hit the floor when Rex bent me over it."

"That devil," The Mistress said as she lightly increased the pressure on Sheridan's clitoris, increased the speed of her movements.

"He was."

"Tell me what you remember feeling. Tell me in detail. And while you're talking, try to remember every sensation he aroused in you..." The Mistress ran a single finger up and down the seam of Sheridan's vagina. "While you remember, imagine yourself getting wetter and wetter, think of all the blood rushing to your labia and your vagina opening…"

Sheridan inhaled slowly and nodded her head. "Yes, Mistress."

"Now keep talking. I might go inside you soon."

The Mistress watched Sheridan's thin fingers dig into the silk of the cushions. But she raised no protest.

"So Rex bent me over this table in the foyer. I remember the cool, slick wood under my right cheek. I held onto the sides as he dragged my panties down my legs."

Again and again, The Mistress ran her finger up and down Sheridan's slit and felt it grow wetter and warmer to the touch.

"And once he had my panties off, he shoved my legs open. Practically kicked them open."

"Wicked man. You must have loved it."

"God, yes. I was scared though. It was all happening so fast, and Rex was pretty big. He could have hurt me if he went in too fast."

"I think most men need the word 'foreplay' tattooed on their cocks. Like a Post-It Note— only permanent."

Sheridan grinned as she lifted her hips a few inches off the pillow. Squirmy thing. Another good sign.

"Truth. But that time Rex managed to control

himself enough. He dropped to his knees and buried his face in me."

"Better. Continue, please."

The Mistress pressed open Sheridan's labia. The girl was soaking wet inside. Gently The Mistress massaged her outer lips in an effort to bring even more blood-flow to her clitoris.

"He attacked me with his tongue, pushed it all the way inside me. It was weird feeling him at that angle. Usually when he went down on me I was on my back, not on my stomach sprawled across a table. But it was good weird, good angle. I got so wet you could hear it when he stuck his fingers in me."

"How many fingers?"

"Three or four. Can't remember. Couldn't tell. They slid right in, I was so wet by then. Slid in deep. He traded off…. He used his fingers on me for a minute or two…then back to oral—he loved to lick me. He'd spread me open really wide and just dive in face first."

"If he loves going down on women, he can't be all that bad."

"He wasn't…really, he wasn't. And sometimes he was even good."

"When he was fucking you?"

"Exactly. Yeah, so he fucked me with his fingers until I was dripping for him."

"You're dripping for me," The Mistress told her with a smile. She still hadn't gone inside

Sheridan yet, wanting to hold off as long as possible.

"I can't remember the last time I was this turned on."

"I know my way around a vagina. Go on with the story."

"So when I was dripping wet for him, he stood up and unbuckled his belt."

"I love that sound."

Sheridan murmured her agreement. "He was good at that too...unbuckling his belt with one hand while his other hand got his cock out..."

The Mistress bit her lip to stifle a laugh. America's Sweetheart had an exquisitely dirty mouth when turned on enough.

"I was dying..." Sheridan said as she moved her hands to her own breasts and began to touch her nipples. "I wanted him inside me so fucking much. No matter how fast he moved, it wasn't fast enough. I think I begged. Out loud maybe. I know I said, 'Please.'"

"Did he please?"

"Oh yeah, he pleased. He pleased hard," Sheridan said with a giggle so amorous she sounded intoxicated. "He slammed into me in one stroke. My hips had bruises on them the next morning from how hard he went it. I kept going to the bathroom just to look at them. He owned me with that thrust."

He owned me... The Mistress had pegged

Sheridan as a submissive. With three words she outed herself.

"On the opposite of the foyer was this big mirror. I remember turning my head and watching him as he fucked me."

"I love doing that. Men think they're the visual ones, but who needs Internet porn when you've got a mirror at the end of your bed?"

"I should get one. God, it was amazing watching him. I'd never done that before really— never watched him while he fucked me. He was almost out of his mind. He wasn't even holding onto me, just the edge of the table. He just…"

Sheridan paused for a breath and to open her thighs even wider. *Good,* The Mistress thought. Sheridan was close to going out of her mind waiting to be penetrated.

"He just pounded me," Sheridan continued. "It was brutal. I heard the table feet scraping the tile floor. And he was grunting and panting like he was in pain almost. You should have seen him…I did see him. I still can see him."

The Mistress let Sheridan fall silent. The girl was no doubt lost in the most erotic memory of her life, the memory of a man so consumed with lust for her he nearly ate her alive in the foyer of his townhouse before he could even be bothered with "hello."

"What else can you see?" The Mistress asked as she opened Sheridan wider and stroked her inner lips. The girl was slick with desire and re-membered passion.

"He grabbed the back of my neck and held me down hard against the table. He was absolutely ramming into me by that point. I don't know…it was like he knew that would be our last time to-gether even though I hadn't told him."

"Did you orgasm then?"

Sheridan shook her head. "No. He came first. Loudly. Usually he was so quiet during sex, really intense. But that time he just groaned. I usually couldn't feel it when he came either, but that night I did. When he pulled out, his cum dribbled down my legs and onto the floor."

"I hope he had a forgiving housekeeper."

"He left me laying on the table while he zipped his pants back up. Then he grabbed me and picked me up. I laughed out loud at that. Crazy. It was so *Gone With the Wind,* him carrying me up the stairs. I told him I could walk."

"You look like you weigh about ninety-five pounds. Let the man carry you."

"I did and I loved it. I loved it when he threw me onto his bed upstairs. And I loved it when he took his belt and whipped the back of my legs with it."

"Ohh…masochistic streak. I can work with that."

"I hope you do, Mistress," Sheridan said, her

voice dropping an octave. "He didn't hit me very often. Didn't want anyone seeing the welts."

"Occupational hazard in my world. Our world," The Mistress corrected. The sooner Sheridan accepted her kinky side, the sooner she'd be able to enjoy sex again.

"Exactly. But I was eighteen then and we were wild that night. He whipped me from ass to ankles…"

"I'm putting that on my To Do List."

"And then he tied to me to the bed on my back. He was already hard again. He crawled on top of me… I loved looking at him. I don't know why but he always wore his suit during sex. Never undressed. He'd take off his jacket, roll up his sleeves, but that was it. He'd leave on the vest or his tie… I loved it though. It felt so dirty being naked while he was fully dressed in his sexy business suits. Maybe that's why he did it."

The Mistress kept her mouth shut. A man in his late thirties, early forties having an affair with a beautiful girl half his age? She knew exactly why he kept his clothes on during sex: he didn't want Sheridan seeing his aging body.

"What did he do then?" The Mistress asked.

"He fucked me again. Not as hard this time. Slower…much slower. It was always slower the second time. And he finally kissed me. And while he was kissing me he started rubbing my clit. That was my favorite…when he touched my clit while inside me. I came every time when he did that."

"Like this?"

The Mistress turned her hand and pushed three fingers deep into Sheridan's body as she carefully rubbed her clitoris with her other hand. As the first penetration, Sheridan gasped and dug her hands back into the cushions.

She nodded mutely. Just like that.

"Keep remembering, Sheridan," The Mistress ordered. "But don't talk. Just remember how good it felt, this man on top of you and inside you and how it felt when you hit that moment when the pressure starts to build and you know if he just keeps doing exactly what he's doing you're going to come and come hard…"

The Mistress pushed the knuckle of her thumb into Sheridan's g-spot and smiled as the girl flinched with pleasure. Sheridan's head fell back and the heels of her shoes dug so hard into the silk cushion that the fabric started to rip. Lost in ecstasy, Sheridan didn't even seem to notice.

A lifetime of experience with the female orgasm had taught The Mistress that all she had to do now was not stop. A red flush spread across Sheridan's chest. Her breathing had quickened wildly. Every muscle in her legs had gone taut. The Mistress pushed in another finger and the girl's body opened to her like a flower. With a little lube, she could have shoved her whole hand into the girl. But they'd save that for next time. Now all that mattered was getting Sheridan to the edge and pushing her over it.

"I want you to come for me, Sheridan. I'm ordering you to come for me. I'm not taking off that blindfold or letting you out of this room until you come for me. I don't care if it takes all night. You can do this."

"I don't know...it's been years. I—"

"It's not you, Sheridan. It's them. The guys you've been with who didn't understand who you are and what you are. You can orgasm. There's nothing wrong with you. They didn't know what they were doing. Vanilla sex with a guy who treats you like his best buddy isn't going to do it for you. And it shouldn't. You deserve better sex than that. You belong at the feet of a man who owns you and treats you like his property and inflicts orgasms on you like a punishment..."

"Oh God..." she panted between breaths.

The Mistress pushed harder onto her clitoris, moved her hand faster and deeper inside her vagina...

"There's nothing wrong with you, Little Miss."

Sheridan's hips rose again off the cushion and hovered a few inches in the air.

"This nothing wrong with you at all," The Mistress said and shoved in once more.

With a loud and lusty cry, Sheridan's back arched, her body froze, and every muscle inside her fluttered wildly, almost painfully around The Mistress's hand as an orgasm years in the making ripped through the girl and sent fluid pouring out of her and onto the red silk.

When the last contraction subsided, The Mistress carefully pulled out of Sheridan and let the girl take a few minutes to breathe.

Sheridan's breathing slowed. The Mistress grinned as a laugh, a beautiful tired laugh, escaped Sheridan's lips, and a smile as wide as the sky spread across her face. Nowhere on the girl's face did The Mistress see shame or self-loathing or fear.

The Mistress reached behind Sheridan's head and untied the blindfold. Sheridan blinked a few times and looked up into The Mistress's eyes.

"I can't believe that happened," she said in a faint whisper. "I haven't come with another person in years."

"Welcome back. Next session, I'll give you two orgasms. But you better tip well."

"God, you're good at this, Mistress."

And for reasons that The Mistress couldn't explain and won't explain and certainly will never apologize for, she gave the girl the quickest of kisses on her lips.

"Told you so."

* * *

Jesus H. Christ, Kingsley. Stop reading over my shoulder. Do you know how hard it is to concentrate with you breathing in my goddamn ear? I can hear your erection.

Kingsley...what are you doing? Stop biting me. I'm still typing here. I'm typing all of this. I want your biting me in the permanent record.

Could someone tell Kingsley to please stop biting me?

Fine. I'll do it myself.

And now you're taking your clothes off.

I love this damn job.

FILE #2

Client Name: Robert Bruce (age 45)

Profession: Above my pay grade

Inclination: Dominant

Level of Experience: Moderate

Orientation: Straight

* * *

Okay, client profile number two coming up right. This one should be a lot easier to write without that nymphomaniac Frenchman Kingsley hanging around. Big mistake trying to write these files at Kingsley's house. The man just cannot keep his nose out of my business sometimes. And by "nose," of course, I mean "penis." And by "my business," I mean…

Well, you know what I mean.

Hello, Dear Reader. I'll assume that if you're reading this file you're also in Kingsley's employ as either a pro-Dom or a pro-sub. He has some ridiculous notion that I am the greatest dominatrix working today and that all pros can learn a thing or two from my interactions with clients. All right, maybe it isn't that ridiculous. I'm pretty damn good at this. What can I say? I learned from the best. But the less said about Him the better.

Back on topic. As you know, Fellow Minions of Kingsley, this job we do is really just a job. Most days at least. We show up. We kick ass (or get our asses kicked—I'm not forgetting you cute little subs out there). We yell, we flog, we insult, we beat and bruise, and then we send them home happy and hand off our 15% to Kingsley.

But some days the job is more than a job. And those are either the best days or the worst days. Some days I'm less a dominatrix and more a therapist. A lot of people come to me already broken and only by breaking them again can they finally heal right. I like those days although they scare the shit out of me. You try never to take the job home with you.

Although, on rare occasions, you go home with the job.

Robert came to The Mistress on a Thursday afternoon during her office hours. Kingsley had
scoffed at the idea of a dominatrix holding a
weekly salon for her clients. Anything that in-
volved kinky people in the same room together
keeping their clothes *on* baffled his poor French
brain. But The Mistress understood that the dy-
namics with her clients changed and their bonds
strengthened when they could interact as domme
and sub without the erotic stress of a scene
looming. The subs brought her their bruises for
inspection and applause. The Doms came to
learn her secrets. One hour a week could breed a
lifetime of well-paid loyalty. The Mistress, as always, knew what she was doing.

When Robert entered the room (Kingsley's
private lounge on the first floor), The Mistress
couldn't quite discern exactly what he wanted
from her. He stood in the corner and watched as

The Mistress rubbed the shoulder of her favorite female submissive. Her Little Miss had played too hard with a sadist the night before and had a pulled muscle to prove it. The Mistress loved to coo over her broken-winged doves. This Little Miss melted into her hands as the sub regaled The Mistress with the story of last night's erotic adventure. Robert listened attentively but without any discernible lascivious intentions. He had the posture and the bearing of a dominant. He stood straight with his chin high, and at no point did he shrink from eye contact. Although the Little Miss at The Mistress's feet told a lurid story of pain and passion (and some double penetration while suspended facedown from the ceiling via a leather harness and some elaborate *Kinbaku*, i.e. Japanese rope bondage—*see attached diagram*), Robert never once batted an eyelash. The story neither repulsed nor astonished him. He listened as if he'd heard the tale before. Or perhaps even lived it.

Curiosity got the better of The Mistress and with a quick kiss, she sent her Little Miss on her way. Alone with Robert at last, she lounged back in the black and gold embroidered armchair, crossed one booted ankle over her bare thigh, and waited for him to speak.

He clearly sensed her interest in him and withheld his words as he sat across from her on the low sofa by the quietly burning fireplace. A handsome man in his forties, he looked just enough like Denzel Washington that The Mistress rather hoped she was wrong about the whole Dom thing. Robert was new to The Mistress, but he must not have been new to Kingsley to be inside the inner sanctum.

"I've heard of you," Robert said as he clasped his large, well-manicured hands by his knees.

"Who hasn't?" The Mistress asked, giving him a smile.

He didn't take the bait and flirt or flatter her. Her estimation of him, already fairly high, inched up further.

"My name is Robert Bruce. I need your help."

"My name is Mistress Nora. I sell help."

"I can pay."

"I know you can. Otherwise King wouldn't have let you in the door. Let's talk about the situation first. I'll write up the invoice later."

Robert sighed and sat back on the sofa. A tall man, he carried himself with dignity, but still The Mistress sensed a struggle within him. Men often came to her at war with their consciences. Society had taught them, and rightly so in most instances, to never lay a hand on a woman. So when dark desires crept into their dreams—desires to tie up a woman and flog her or spank her, beat her and bruise her even as she begged for more—they came to The Mistress for absolution.

Absolution wasn't her area...but she could show them how to throw a flogger like a pro.

"I'm married," Robert finally spoke again.

"My sympathies."

He laughed then, a rich warm laugh and The Mistress wrinkled her nose at him by way of apology.

"I actually like being married, Mistress. Love it even."

"Fascinating. You're here because of your wife?"

"Yes, she...she's something, my Cara." The smile left his mouth and moved to his ebony eyes. The Mistress saw love in that smile, love in those eyes. Married and in love? The Mistress was half-tempted to take a blood sample from the man and send it to the labs.

"She must be to put that rise in your Levis."

Robert sat up straighter and gave The Mistress a wide-eyed stare.

"Don't worry, Robert. If there aren't at least three men in this house at any one time walking around with full erections, Kingsley calls a staff meeting. You love your wife. She must be incredibly beautiful to get you in a manly way by just thinking about her. I might have to meet this woman."

"I want you to meet her." Robert pulled one of the gold pillows across his lap. "I can't really bring her here. Not yet anyway."

"Do you want me to meet your wife? Or do you want me to beat your wife?"

Robert exhaled heavily. He rubbed his forehead and gave a short rueful laugh. "She wants *me* to beat her."

"And you don't want to do it?"

"No. Hell no. I'd love to. It's just…"

The Mistress waited. From the moment she saw Robert standing in the corner, she knew her day was about to get interesting. She did so love interesting days.

"Just what, Robert?" The Mistress leaned forward and let one lace-encased arm drape over the other as she studied him. Her breasts were on ample display in her black-and-white-striped corset. But Robert only looked into her eyes.

"Just…I'm afraid to ask for this. It's crazy. I know you'll say no."

He paused for a breath. Whatever he was about to ask clearly required as much courage as the man had within him. The Mistress couldn't wait to hear what perverted, sadistic, terrifying plan the man had in mind.

"Will you come home with me and meet my wife?" he said.

"You sick, twisted motherfucker."

Robert blanched. The Mistress laughed.

"Come on," she said, throwing her toy bag over her shoulder. "I'll drive."

* * *

The Mistress drove and Robert sat in the passenger seat eyeing her warily.

"What? Did you think I'd say no?" The Mistress asked.

"I assumed you would. Isn't coming home with clients a little…"

"It's not usually done, no. But I'm not your ordinary dominatrix. I make ten times what my sisters in sadism do because I do the stuff they won't. Like…"

"Go to client's houses?"

"For starters. Now tell me how you know Kingsley. You must know Kingsley somehow."

"I know Kingsley."

"Carnal knowledge?"

"He wishes."

"I like you, Robert Bruce. Keep talking."

Robert toyed with his watchband as The Mistress took them to the edge of Manhattan.

"Don't do that," she said. "You're not the fidgeting type. It hurts my soul to see a dignified Dom fidgeting."

"Sorry, Mistress. How do you know I'm a Dom though?"

"I'll eat my own underwear if you're a sub. Switch? Maybe, although you seem like a man of hard and simple desires. Switches are much more flighty and fucked up. I know this from experience. So Dom?"

"Yes. Ex-Dom."

"Future Dom. You've topped before?"

"Old girlfriend," Robert explained. "She got me into it back when I was in grad school. MBA."

"MBA? I stand corrected. You're obviously a masochist. Continue."

"Not much to tell. She was one of Kingsley's crew back then. That's how I know him."

"True love?"

"Yeah...for about six months. Loved her with all my cock and soul."

"How romantic."

Robert laughed at himself. "She was kinky as hell. Been in the scene since she was a teenager. Told me I couldn't lay a hand on her without tying her up first. She gave me the basic tour of BDSM. After a couple nights, she called me a natural."

"I can see that. So Cock and Soul girl? She went by the wayside?"

"Wasn't meant to be. Met my Cara a few years later. Real true love. Married. One little one. Not so little really. He's nine now."

"Hope he's not home. I tend to scare children. On purpose."

"No, he's not home. At his grandmother's.

Thursday night is our night. Cara and I always make sure we have our private time."

"You two are so damn cute. I can't even guess what the problem is here. Is there really a problem, or are you just trying to trick me into participating in some sort of unholy threesome with whips and chains and butt-plugs as big as bugles? I'm fine with either really."

Robert chuckled again, nervously this time, and The Mistress heard a note of real distress in that too-casual laugh.

"There's a problem, I promise."

* * *

They took the elevator in Robert's building up to a pleasantly understated penthouse apartment (or as understated as a two-million-dollar penthouse apartment could be). The Mistress watched as Robert took off his shoes and sat them on a bench by the door. The furniture, plush and monochromatic, sat arrayed in symmetrical lines. Nothing seemed out of place. She'd never seen a home more scrupulously tidy before. Not even a stray shoe littered the floor.

"Your wife is either OCD or some sort of serial killer. I can't wait to meet her." The Mistress hoisted her toy bag high on her shoulder.

"The wife can't wait to meet you either," came a voice from the kitchen.

A lovely woman of about thirty-five emerged from an open doorway and smiled blankly toward Nora's voice. She had sleek red hair cut into a simple bob and wore no makeup other than a splash of pale pink lip-gloss.

"I promise the wife is neither OCD nor a serial killer," Cara—the wife—said, holding out her hand in The Mistress's general direction. Her eyes looked past, not at, The Mistress's face. "In fact, the wife is…"

"The wife is blind," The Mistress said, shaking hands with the woman.

"That she is," Cara said with a wide grin.

Robert put his arm around Cara's shoulder. "Now do you see the problem?"

The Mistress looked Cara up and down. Beautiful woman—pale skin, ample curves, a beauty mark at the corner of her mouth…and pale hazel eyes that stared unseeing at nothing and no one.

"Nope. I don't see a problem at all," said The Mistress.

"I definitely don't see a problem," Cara added.

"Funny and blind. I like this wife of yours. Now…is there any booze in this house?"

Robert led them into the kitchen and told The Mistress to have a seat. Once the wine was poured, an awkward silence descended over the three of them. The Mistress loved awkward silences. She liked to create them on purpose sometimes, just to see who would break the silence first. Tonight she put her mental money on Cara.

Cara was smart money.

"He worries too much about me. That's the real problem." Cara took a sip of her wine only after speaking, as if to prove she didn't need the liquid courage.

Robert laid his large hand on his wife's thin forearm before reaching up to touch her face. The Mistress noted the gesture. He'd done the same thing earlier before putting his arm around her. He must touch her arm first to give her fair warning of his proximity before touching more of her. Over-protective indeed.

"Cara, you're blind," he said. "I feel like I have to remind you of this more often than I should."

"I wasn't born blind," Cara said, turning her head, if not her eyes, toward The Mistress.

"What happened?" The Mistress asked, and Robert shifted in his chair.

"Accident," Cara explained. "I was nineteen. Standing on a street corner—"

"Hooking. Got it."

"Hey—" Robert interrupted angrily, but Cara only laughed and patted Robert's hand.

"Yes. I was turning tricks on the way to class," Cara continued with a grin. "And someone bumped into me. Just an accident. No malice. Went down and hit the back of my head on the curb. Slammed my occipital lobe. The lights went out and they never came back on again."

"Incredible…" The Mistress exhaled. "One question."

"Of course."

"Did that help or hinder your prostitution career?"

Cara burst out laughing as Robert buried his head on his wife's shoulder.

"She's fun, Robert," Cara said. "Let's keep her."

"She's a little out of our price range for full-time employment." Robert kissed Cara quick on the cheek.

"Is she pretty?" Cara asked Robert. "She sounds pretty."

"I'm hideous. I look like a shaved Muppet."

"Robert?" Cara prompted.

"She's the second most beautiful woman in the entire city," Robert said. "White girl. Long black hair. Wavy. She's got part of it pulled back but it still looks a little messy—sexy and wild. She's short, although her boots put a few inches on her. Curvy but muscular. Fantastic breasts especially in that corset. Green eyes. About…thirty. Total goddess."

"Thank you, darling," Cara said.

"Wait. This is your husband's job?" The Mistress asked. "To describe women to you? This is a damn good gig."

"Since I wasn't blind from birth, I can still visualize people. Old habits die hard." Cara turned her head to Robert. "I try to guess what people look like by their voices and personalities. Then Robert tells me if I'm right or not."

"He probably lies to you constantly," The Mistress said before taking another sip of her wine. "I would."

"I do," Robert admitted. "She doesn't even know I'm Black."

"Great. Now she does." The Mistress rolled her eyes.

"My parents are going to be shocked," Cara said, trying to keep a straight face. "What will we tell the children?"

"We have more than one child?"

"You're not the only one with secrets, dear."

The Mistress sat back in her chair and studied the playfully bickering spouses. Rarely had she seen a couple so comfortably in love with each other. Something ached inside her at the sight of such easy affection. She'd had this once, this kind of perfect peace. A name she tried to never speak echoed in the empty parts of her, reverberating off the hollow walls of her heart.

"Yes, well," The Mistress said when the cuteness had reached its zenith. "This is all well and good, but if I'm here, then someone has got to

get their ass kicked tonight. Do we have any vol-
unteers?"

Cara's hand shot up straight in the air. Robert
reached up, gently clasped her wrist, and pulled
her hand back down.

The Mistress shook her head in disgust.
"Now that was uncalled for."

"Mistress, Cara is blind. Completely. You
don't go around beating up blind women. Especially not when the blind woman happens to be
my wife."

"Your wife clearly wants to be beaten," The
Mistress reminded him. "Remember this?" The
Mistress threw her arm up in the air and waved
it eagerly. "You should. It happened like seven
seconds ago."

"Yes, you should, Robert," Cara said, an edge
of irritation in her voice. "I want it."

"You only you think you want it. You're just
curious because we ran into Toni last week."

"Toni was your kinky ex-girlfriend?" The Mistress's ears perked up at that. "Not *the* Toni? Toni
the sexy masochist who used to sleep with
Kingsley? And by 'sleep,' I mean anything but
sleep?"

"She also used to sleep with me," Robert admitted with a sheepish shrug of his broad shoulders. "And we did actually sleep sometimes."

"God. Damn. You used fuck Toni the Tiger.
That girl scared half the sadists in The Under-

ground. I saw her play human pincushion during an erotic acupuncture play scene once. She didn't even bleed. You must be even more hardcore than I pegged you for."

The Mistress turned to Cara: "I mean 'pegged' metaphorically. I haven't pegged your husband. That costs extra."

"Understandably," Cara said, nodding. "Here's the thing, Mistress. He is hardcore. We ran into this Toni woman and I could hear her drooling over him. I grilled him that night. I wanted to know everything. I'm not jealous at all. Really."

The Mistress raised an eyebrow. "Really."

"Fine. I am jealous. Not that he had a relationship with her, but that he had *that kind of* relationship with her, and he won't have it with me."

"And you want something like that too?" The Mistress finished for her.

Robert groaned.

"None of that," The Mistress waved her hand at him in a scolding. "The Mistress is talking to the sub in the room right now. You just sit there and look pretty. Cara, why do you want that kind of relationship? Just curiosity?"

"No. I mean, yes. I mean, yes I'm curious. I've never done it before. But I've had fantasies about it since I was a teenager and found my mom's stash of smut."

"God, I love smut. Let me guess...the *Sleeping Beauty* trilogy?"

Cara's mouth fell open just slightly. "Yes! How did you—"

"Seriously, I should start sending a cut of my checks to Anne Rice. I owe that woman half my clients. But come on now. Surely it's more than that."

Cara exhaled heavily and crossed her arms over her chest. "It's more than that. Robert...he takes such good care of me. So protective. I swear he'd lay down his jacket over mud puddles I have to cross if I'd let him. Just once in a while, I wish he wasn't so protective of me. He loves me like a wife, yes. But sometimes he treats me like a child."

"I have heard this story before," The Mistress said, smiling.

"And maybe if he treated me like he did Toni, if he saw me like he saw her...I don't know. I just want to try. I want to be a woman to him—a whole woman. A woman he's not afraid to treat like a woman, and not like his fragile blind wife who needs saved."

"Robert, are you hearing all of this?" The Mistress asked, turning her attention to him.

Robert looked up at the ceiling. "Yes, Mistress."

"Good man. Is any of this sinking in? Or at the very least, giving you a semi?"

"Yes, Mistress." He rubbed his face and laughed. "I want to make her happy."

"It can't just be about her though. You have to want to do this. You have to want to top her. You can't just go through the motions or she'll know it. You enjoyed what you did with Toni, right?"

Robert glanced at Cara, who clearly sensed his diffidence to answer even though she couldn't see it.

"It's fine." Cara found Robert's hand and squeezed it. "I wasn't a virgin when we met. I had boyfriends I loved being with before you. You're allowed to have fond memories of ex-girl-friends."

Robert raised Cara's hand and kissed it. "I wouldn't trade a thousand nights with Toni for five minutes with you, my love." He kissed her hand once more. "But yes, I loved topping Toni in the beginning. She loved pain, loved being used and abused. The sex was never rough enough for her. At first it's a sexy challenge. But then it got old. I love playing Dom but not every night."

"I don't want every night either," Cara said. "I love our sex life. But I do want to do this tonight. And if we both enjoy it maybe again in a week or two."

"Do you want some help here?" The Mistress offered. The more they kept talking, the greater the risk Robert would chicken out. They needed to get started doing. "I can play wingman. The first scene's always the hardest. I've got floggers with me, some cuffs and stuff. We can do this together."

Robert put his hand on Cara's shoulder. "Would you be comfortable with The Mistress watching and helping?"

"She'll keep her clothes on, won't she?" Cara asked Robert.

"I'm already naked," The Mistress said. "Bedroom, perverts. Now. I have an idea."

"I'm going to admit to being terrified by your idea," Robert said as he ushered The Mistress and Cara into the master bedroom, which was perfectly named. Perhaps Robert hadn't consciously decorated his bedroom to look like a dungeon, but it certainly gave off a darkly erotic air. The king-sized bed was draped in black and white linens. The four-poster bed frame was constructed of sturdy metal bars tailor-made for restraining a willing submissive. The walls were painted a deep red. Low leather chairs sat under the windows that overlooked the streets. The Mistress couldn't help but picture a naked, helpless Cara with her legs draped over each chair arm, her owner violating her with his fingers and mouth as the whole city watched.

"You should be terrified of my idea," The

Mistress said. "It's pure evil genius, just like me. Now Cara…"

The Mistress stood in front of Robert's wife and took her hands. Cara had already begun to pant a little in both in nervousness and anticipation.

The Mistress continued, "I'm going to talk Robert through this. You're not going to hear a word I say. Once the scene starts, only he can hear my voice. You'll just ignore it. It's background music and that's all. You'll only listen to your husband. You'll do everything he tells you to do without question. You're his sexual property. Aren't you?"

"Yes, Mistress," Cara whispered.

Out of the corner of her eyes, The Mistress saw Robert stand up straighter. "You love him. You trust him. You belong to him. He's going to flog you and he's going to fuck you. And you're…?"

Cara's face broke into a wide grin. "Going to love it."

"Did you hear that, Robert?" The Mistress asked.

"Oh, I heard that. Every part of my body heard that."

"I might help Robert. I might even touch you. But it'll merely be an extension of him. Are you comfortable with that?"

"Very, Mistress."

"Good. Now for Kink 101, Cara. You're going to get a beating and it's going to hurt. You'll say ow and no and that's fine. You're getting flogged. It's supposed to hurt. If you don't want Robert to stop, you need a safe word so you can keep up with your 'oh, ah, ow, shit, fuck, damn that hurts,' and he'll keep on flogging. So pick a word you'll remember that wouldn't possibly cross your lips unless you were one-hundred percent certain you wanted the scene to stop."

"Um...suggestions?"

"What's your favorite guilty pleasure food?"

"I don't know. Popcorn?"

"Don't insult me."

"Okay. Funyuns."

"Disgusting. And perfect. Funyuns it is. Let's do this. Don't be afraid. Just have fun."

"Having fun already."

"Now, Robert...what do you want Cara to call you? Sir? Master? Daddy?"

"Daddy?" he asked with some horror.

"Don't judge."

"I think 'sir' has the least amount of baggage here."

"Good choice. 'Sir' is a classic. Let's get started. Cara, take your clothes off and kneel on the bed. We're going to leave the room while you undress. Robert will come back in and that's when the scene will start. You'll be safe. You'll be protected. You'll get your ass kicked. Sound good?"

"Sounds perfect."

"This way, Sir," The Mistress said as she took Robert by the arm and led him from the room.

Once outside the bedroom, The Mistress closed the door to let Cara have a last moment of privacy, and also to give Robert a few extra minutes of mental preparation. "You can do this," she told him.

"I can do this. I can't do this."

The Mistress slapped him hard on the side of the arm. Robert winced and mouthed an "ow."

"Did that hurt?" she asked.

"Yes, it did."

"Is it going to kill you?"

"No…"

"There. That's why you're doing to Cara. Just giving her some *thwaps*. It'll hurt. It won't cause a bit of harm. If she ends up with even a bruise after this, I'll be surprised. I've got light floggers great for beginners. You know what you're doing. If you used to top Toni then I know you know what you're doing."

"I know what I'm doing. It's just…" Robert paused and took a deep breath. His face clouded over with both love and concern. "My wife is blind, Mistress. She is blind. She can't see anything. She can't protect herself. When she goes out alone, I'm a wreck until she gets back. She could get hurt so easily. Anything...a break in the concrete, a piece of trash on the ground, a dog off his leash...or worse. A mugger...a rapist...anything."

"But you let her go, right?"

"Well, yeah. I can't make her my prisoner. She's an adult, after all. She'd divorce me if I treated her like a child in need of constant protection."

"You treat her like an adult outside the bedroom. Now you're just going to do it inside the bedroom. And I have something that will help."

"More alcohol?"

"Better. Let's go. She should be naked by now." The Mistress clapped her hands together and rubbed them with maniacal glee in the hopes of getting a laugh out of Robert. He did laugh, but he didn't sound like he meant it.

The Mistress put her hands on his face and forced him to meet her eyes. "Trust me, Robert. I know what I'm doing. Say that you trust me."

"I trust you, Mistress."

"Good. Now let's go beat and fuck your wife."

The Mistress took Robert by the shoulders and spun him toward the bedroom door. When he touched the knob, The Mistress spoke one last word of warning to him.

"Don't be afraid. And if you are, don't act like it. Got me?"

"Yes, Mistress."

"Let's do it."

* * *

Robert opened the door and inhaled sharply when he saw Cara kneeling naked at the edge of the bed. She was a sight to behold with her dark red hair coming just to the top of her long elegant naked neck. Impossible to believe the woman had carried a child once. She had smooth creamy skin, a taut body, and full, high breasts. Only her softly rounded stomach betrayed her age and experience.

"My God..." Robert whispered at the doorway, whispered so quietly only The Mistress could hear. "That's my wife."

"Your wife and your property. Go claim her."

Nodding, Robert headed toward the bed with eager footsteps. He started to reach out for Cara's hand that rested on top of her thigh.

"Is that the part of her you really want to touch?" The Mistress asked softly as she stood at his side.

"I always—"

"I know. You always touch her hand before you touch any other part of her. She's your property. You own her whole body and can use it any way you want. You don't have to pussyfoot around your own property. Touch her how you want to touch her, not how you think you should touch her."

Robert pulled his hand back. The Mistress watched. She knew this was the crucial moment, the moment when Robert would either reclaim his bedroom dominance or remain a scared, vanilla husband.

"You own her," The Mistress reminded him. Cara stayed still with her eyes closed. She seemed to be holding her breath.

"Yes," he said and gripped his wife by the back of the neck. "Yes, I do."

The Mistress would have applauded, but she was too busy enjoying the show.

Cara gasped as Robert brought his mouth down hard onto her shoulder and bit into the soft skin. He stood behind her and cupped both breasts in his hands. Soft murmurs of pleasure escaped Cara's lips. The Mistress bent and opened her toy bag. She pulled out one special item and held it out in front of Cara's face.

"What is that?" Robert asked, eyeing the object.

"Blindfold. Use it."

"But—"

"I told you to trust me." The Mistress gave him her steadiest, most commanding stare. Robert took the black silk blindfold and wrapped it around Cara's eyes and tied it at the back of her head. Cara smiled with silent understanding.

"Now your wife isn't blind anymore. She's just blindfolded."

Robert looked at The Mistress for a long quiet moment. He mouthed a mute "thank you." The Mistress merely bowed her head toward the blindfolded Cara.

"Do it," The Mistress ordered.

He did it.

Robert's ex-lover Toni had loved being blindfolded. Anything to intensify a scene. He was used to this, dominating a woman in a blindfold. Now the reason Cara couldn't see had nothing to do with an accident and injury. Now she couldn't see because Robert had blindfolded her. He owned all her body now, even her eyes.

Without any further diffidence or hesitation, Robert took control of Cara's body. He slid his hands down her chest and held her breasts again. Her nipples went hard at his touch. One hand slid further down and found her clitoris nestled inside the soft red curls at the apex of her thighs. He kneaded it gently as Cara began to moan and move her hips.

"You like that, don't you?" Robert rasped the words into Cara's ear.

"Yes, Sir."

"You're a slut for my touch, aren't you?" He punctuated the question with another bite on her neck.

"Only yours, Sir."

"Better be." He took her by the shoulder and pushed her forward onto the bed. Robert knelt between her legs and shoved her thighs open with his knees. "I know this is mine and nobody else's."

He reached between her legs and shoved two thick fingers into her. Cara clung to the sheets even as she raised her hips to take him deeper. He fucked her with his hand for a few minutes, digging into her as she writhed and squirmed with need.

"I think you might like that too much," Robert said as he pulled his hand out of her. "I don't think you've earned an orgasm yet, have you?"

He gave her a viciously hard spank that left even The Mistress flinching. The Mistress gave him two thumbs up. She knew a nice hit when she saw it. And the bright red handprint on Cara's bottom certainly testified to the force of that blow.

"No, Sir. But I want to earn it," Cara said as Robert bodily flipped her onto her back.

"Pleasure's earned with pain. You ready to earn it? Don't answer. I don't care if you're ready or not."

The Mistress nodded her approval as Robert dragged Cara off the bed and pulled her to her feet. Back into her toy bag she dove and came out holding a set of dark leather wrist cuffs and a snap hook.

"I think you know what to do with these."

Robert did. He took the cuffs and buckled them onto Cara's wrists. Using the snap hook, he locked her arms high above her head over the top bar of the canopy bed. Good thing Cara was nearly as tall as her husband. Still, she had to strain to stay on her toes. It had to be uncomfortable for her. Good.

The Mistress handed Robert a light flogger. It would sting nicely but not cause too much of a shock. Better to break a new sub in slowly. She'd learned that lesson the hard way.

With a possessive hand, Robert caressed Cara's unmarked back, her full hips and bottom, her long shapely thighs. He glanced at The Mistress once and she winked at him.

"Turn that white girl red," she said by way of encouragement. It was all the encouragement he needed.

He took his stance behind Cara, raised the flogger over his head, and hit clean and hard right at the center of her back. Cara gasped and flinched. Robert gave no quarter. Another hit followed on the heels of the first one. And another and another. He worked his way down her back and up again.

"Like riding a bike," The Mistress said with an approving courtesy clap. The man might not have flogged a woman in ten years but he still had the chops for it.

He aimed lower and struck the sides of her hips, her bottom, and the back of her thighs before making the circuit again. Cara moaned in the back of her throat, cried out a time or two, but she never uttered her safe word or begged for mercy.

When a strike to her thigh unleashed an expletive-laden protest, Robert immediately ceased the flogging. The Mistress tensed. Pain was par for the course in S&M scenes. A dominant couldn't afford to have a weak stomach with a submissive who wanted the real deal. It hurt. Of course it hurt. That was the point after all.

"Do you think you've had enough pain?" Robert asked, the flogger still aloft. "Answer me."

"Yes, Sir," Cara panted, trying to sag into her bonds but not able to.

"Really? Because I don't." Robert let one more strike fall hard and fast and right on her ass. The Mistress beamed with pride.

Then and only then did Robert drop the flogger. Once more he ran his hands over his wife's body.

"You're bright red from your neck to your knees," he said into her ear. "You remember what bright red looks like, don't you?"

"I remember," she said, smiling at his touch.

"Maybe next time I'll turn you black and blue to go along with your red."

"I'd like that, Sir. If I can't see colors, I'd at least like to be colors."

"That's my girl." He slapped her bottom right on the reddest spot and she released another cry of pain and shock. Reaching up, he released the snap hook and her arms fell to her sides. Cara herself nearly fell to the floor, but Robert caught her just in time. He picked her up and threw her roughly onto the bed. While she grimaced in discomfort from her welts, Robert positioned her between the bedposts, her hips right at the edge of the mattress.

"Rope," he said to The Mistress with the authority of a doctor demanding a scalpel from his faithful nurse.

"Coming right up."

The Mistress dug into her toy bag and pulled out two lengths of silk rope. While Robert tied Cara's right ankle to one bedpost, The Mistress tied her left ankle to the other. Her legs formed a V. She couldn't close her thighs to hide herself even if she wanted to. And as wet as she appeared, Cara clearly didn't want to.

"What would you suggest I do to this little slut of mine, Mistress?" Robert asked, giving his wife an appraising look.

"She did take the beating beautifully. Perhaps she's earned a little of this." The Mistress pulled a large phallic-shaped vibrator out of her bag and covered it in a condom.

"Or maybe a lot of this..." Robert took the vibrator, turned it on to a medium setting, and pressed it to Cara's clitoris. She flinched again, but this time in obvious pleasure.

"Shall I help make this more interesting?" The Mistress offered, pulling a set of nipple clamps from her bag.

"By all means."

The Mistress ran a hand over Cara's breast while Robert continued to massage her clitoris and outer labia with the vibrator while she pleaded for penetration. Such a tease. He was damn good at this.

With fingers that knew exactly how to touch a woman, The Mistress kneaded Cara's nipple until it swelled and hardened. She carefully applied one nipple clamp and let it dangle provocatively from her breast. The other nipple clamp provoked an even stronger reaction.

* * *

"I have rope and clothespins if you get in the mood for a zipper." The Mistress gazed mischievously at Robert.

"We'll have to save something for next time. Zipper sounds good for a second session."

"A zipper?" Cara asked, her voice flush with

fear and desire, a combination The Mistress had come to think of as the sound of submission.

Robert pressed the tip of the vibrator an inch into his wife.

"You get thin rope and thread it through clothespins," he explained. "You take the clothespins and put them all over the sub's body. Then you take the end of the rope and yank. It's excruciating."

"I do them all the time," The Mistress said. "I'll even give you my spare bag of pins. You know...for next time."

Cara shivered, but The Mistress couldn't tell if it was from fear or pleasure. Probably both.

"You're about to kill your poor wife, you know?" The Mistress nodded toward the area of erotic torture.

"Well...I am pretty fond of her. Can't have her dying," Robert said before plunging the vibrator deep into her.

Something bordering on a scream of ecstasy emanated from Cara's throat loud enough to send both Robert and The Mistress laughing. Inflicting pleasure could be nearly as enjoyable as inflicting pain. And often just as humiliating for the writhing submissive.

Robert fucked his wife long and hard with the vibrator, plunging it into her over and over again. He pushed the tip into her g-spot, shoved it deep into the back of her vagina, and pulled it out to massage her labia once more. As much as she panted and moaned, Robert didn't let her orgasm. Vicious man. The Mistress wanted to give him a medal.

"You want to come, don't you?" Robert demanded as his wife's hips moved in desperate undulations.

"Yes. Please, Sir," she begged. The Mistress heard real need in her voice.

"I'll let you. But not with this. You come on my cock alone."

"I want it so much." Cara's fingers dug into the sheets and a series of barely articulate "pleases" escaped her lips.

"Keep begging and you might," Robert said as he untied Cara's ankles from the bedposts. He grabbed her arms and pushed her onto her stomach and then pulled her legs to the floor.

"Please, Sir…" Cara said as she spread her thighs wider and lifted her hips by way of invitation. Robert slapped her hard on the bottom again, and she inhaled in surprise. The Mistress could tell Cara wasn't used to being touched by Robert without any sort of warning. She seemed to like it.

Robert opened his pants and gripped his wife by her hips. Every inch of him disappeared into her wet and waiting body. As he thrust into her, Robert ran his hands over Cara's back, which was now marbled with red welts. He touched them lovingly, tenderly even as he pounded deep into her without mercy.

After a minute or two, he pulled out and forced Cara onto her back again. Her ankles met his shoulders, and his hands held her thighs as he entered her once more.

"Nice. Deep penetration," The Mistress said, leaning casually against the bedpost and thoroughly enjoying the show. "Are you trying to give her cervix a black eye or just going for a blowjob from the other direction?"

Robert took the hint and lowered Cara's legs, letting her wrap them around his back. He slipped a hand between their bodies and teased her clitoris with his fingertips. Cara groaned with pleasure. She found his forearms and held onto them as he pushed into her.

Robert gazed down at his wife's face through half-closed eyes.

"You have a beautiful piece of property there," The Mistress told him, following his eyes to Cara's writhing body.

"I know it," he said as he traced a faint scar on Cara's stomach, the product of a long-ago C-section. The Mistress looked away a moment as Robert bent to kiss his wife on the mouth. The sex she didn't mind watching. But a kiss, that was personal.

The kiss ended but Robert kept his mouth near her mouth.

"I want you to come for me," he said. "And I want to look at all of you while you come. Say, 'Yes, Sir.'"

"Yes, Sir," she breathed.

Robert gathered her close and lifted her as she wrapped her legs and arms around him. He sat on the edge of the bed and rolled back, Cara straddling his hips. She started to move against him, her hands searching his body until they found his chest. At first she moved slowly, clearly relishing the position, the angle, the pleasant press of his body against her clitoris. She ground against him, moving in ovals. Robert teased her nipples, tugging lightly on the clamps as Cara started to push faster. With hunger and frenzy, she rode her husband with animal need. Her breathing grew loud and came in short, quick puffs.

"Do it, Cara," he said in a stern voice. "Come for me. Come right now."

Her body rocked wildly. She dug her fingers in the fabric of his shirt. Her head fell back and with a strangled grunt she came loud and hard. Hard enough even Robert groaned.

She collapsed onto Robert's chest but she didn't stay there long. Robert rolled her off him and positioned Cara onto her hands and knees, entering her from behind in one quick motion.

Once inside her, he didn't thrust. Instead, he stayed still as he jerked Cara's hips against him with bruising precision. The Mistress had seen true masochists who would have tapped out by now from the sheer brute force of the fucking. But Cara seemed to glory in it, groaning and gasping in pleasure until Robert let go and finally came inside her with a few final thrusts.

He pulled out of her and rolled onto his side with an exhausted sigh. Laughing, Cara joined him as Robert dragged her to him. As he kissed her shoulders, he untied the blindfold and tossed it aside. Gently he removed the clamps from her breasts and massaged her sore nipples. The Mistress picked up the discarded toys and put them in her bag. She'd clean them at the dungeon and put them to good and bad use again very soon.

Hefting her toy bag over her shoulder, she gave Robert a wink and left the bedroom. But she didn't make it out of the house before she heard footsteps behind her.

"Mistress?"

The Mistress turned around to find a sweaty, happy, barefoot Robert trailing her.

"You should be spooning your wife right now," she told him. "Go. Scoot. I'll send you a bill."

"That was the best sex I've ever had in my life."

"Congrats. I make a great wingman, don't I?"

"The best. The blindfold...the lectures... I'm adding a big tip. You earned it."

"Why yes, yes I did. Speaking of tips...she's just had her first scene ever. This is a big damn deal. She'll need a lot of aftercare. Hold her a long time. Tell her you're proud of her. Hell, rock her if she likes that sort of thing. Then give her a long hot bath. No more playing. If you want to fuck her again, fine. Just go easy—bondage at most. No more hitting. Also...tell her you love her and that she's your prized possession. Tell her that a lot. Every day even..."

The Mistress said and heard those words ringing in her ears. Someone had said that to her a long time ago, and the echo of them had never fully dissipated.

"I will," he said. "Promise. And I guess I need to get one of those." He nodded at her toy bag.

"No need. Neckties make good blindfolds. Garbage bags are great for tying up wrists and ankles. Spatula for a paddle. Well...I better leave this with you. Not easy to MacGyver a decent flogger."

The Mistress took out the light flogger and handed it to Robert.

"Thank you...for everything," he said.

"Don't thank me," The Mistress said as she opened the door and stepped into the hallway. "The flogger's going on your bill."

* * *

Whew. Robert and Cara. I didn't see them after that. Not together anyway. Robert could handle Cara just fine on his own. But every now and then, he'd show up during my office hours and ask for some suggestions. I taught him my trick for the perfect zipper, gave him some hints on how to tie better knots, helped him trade up to a heavier class of floggers.

Like I said, I never went home with them again. But sometimes when the job gets too dark, too difficult, too ugly, I unpack my memories of them, of their love for each other, and bring them home with me.

FILE #3

Client Name: Dante Burns* (age 29)

Profession: Rock star, lead singer of The Black Sheets

Inclination: Submissive

Level of Experience: None

Orientation: Straight

If that's his real name, I'll eat my little red riding crop

* * *

Okay, King. You're going to love this one. Don't pretend you weren't drooling over this guy when he walked into Headquarters. We all were. Lean but muscular, perfect bed head, two full sleeves of tattoos, big damn smile...remember him?

He came to you with a stack of Benjamins an inch high and a request for "a couple hours with your hottest dominatrix." I remember it well. Not that I was eavesdropping from the next room or anything. I just happened to be in the next room standing by the door with my eye at the keyhole.

What? I was practicing picking locks.

You told him that you had the perfect dominatrix to meet all his needs. Beautiful, intelligent, extremely experienced, and ready and willing to perform any sort of sadistic service for him.

Of course you were talking about me.

Dante said he merely wanted a tour of The Underground.

"We're making a video," he said. "It'll be kinky, something like old Nine Inch Nails. Like the vid for 'Closer' but with fewer dead pigs. I'm not into any of this stuff—the ball-gags and riding crops—but it makes for good visuals. Seriously...I'm not one of those guys. We're just scouting locations."

Yeah sure, kid. And I'm the Virgin Mary.

The Mistress had every right to be skeptical. First of all, while she didn't know much about the music industry, she was fairly certain the lead singers of world-famous, award-winning, many-times platinum-selling bands didn't do their own location scouting for music videos. Maybe Dante was something of a diva who demanded control over every aspect of his band's career trajectory. Certainly plausible. Perhaps he genuinely did want to try his hand at directing and producing, which is why he'd taken this task upon himself.

Whatever the reason he'd come knocking on Kingsley's door, The Mistress really didn't care. He'd paid twice her usual rate for nothing but a tour of the dungeons, the clubs, and a couple hours of picking her brain about the job. Easy money, right?

Not quite.

The Mistress met Dante in Kingsley's office. From the moment their eyes met and she shook his hand, she had a hunch about him. The second she appeared, Kingsley seemingly disappeared to Dante. Not once did Dante glance at Kingsley after The Mistress made her entrance.

"So you're The Mistress?" Dante's eyes grazed her body from head to boot and back again. "Very nice to meet you."

"Very nice to beat you," she said, giving him her most dangerous sort of grin.

"No beating." He wagged his finger at her like a teacher to a naughty pupil. For a split second, she considered how much force she'd have to exert to break that finger. "Here for the tour and nothing more."

"Yes, for your music video, you said. How nice. We lifestyle dominants love it when outsiders take our entire world, our culture, and our

people and turn it all into a fake Hollywood bub-
blegum backdrop for a pop song."

She said with words with a smile and enjoyed
watching Dante squirm in his punk boots.

"It's more alternative than pop," he said
sheepishly. "Really good alternative. My band's
hardcore."

"Hardcore? So am I. Poured scalding candle-
wax on a client's balls yesterday. Your band does
that sort of thing?"

"Um..." Dante went pale underneath his tan.
"We say fuck a lot."

"Yeah, so did my grandmother."

"Maîtresse?" Kingsley gave her a stern stare.
She only winked at him. "This is Dante Burns.
He's been hailed as the next Trent Reznor."

"Who?"

"You don't know who Trent Reznor is?"
Dante said, sounding aghast.

"Is he a client, King?"

"*Non.*"

"Have I ever fucked him?" she asked.

"Not to my knowledge," Kingsley said. "His
band, Nine Inch Nails—"

"Not ringing a bell. Sorry." She turned to
Dante and shook his hand. "So you're the next
Someone-I've-Never-Heard-Of. Congrats."

Dante looked heartbroken. Poor baby.

The Mistress took her hand back. "King? We
good to go?"

Kingsley stared at her with wide eyes, then waved them from the office. The stack of hundreds on his desk would go long ways toward taking care of the headache she'd just given him.

"Ready, Mr. Burns?"

"Sure." He sounded doubtful now. Gone was the cocky rock star. "I'm all yours."

He said the words casually, too casually. Behind them she heard something. Something hungry, something wistful, something true.

"This is HQ," The Mistress said as they left Kingsley's office. "Kingsley lives here, works here, and reigns here. He takes the King part of Kingsley very seriously. You should too. You might be more famous than he is and you might even have more money, but there's no one in the house who would take your side against him, who would take an order from you that he had contradicted, who would even take a step out of this house with you without his permission."

"Seriously?"

"Seriously. King doesn't have employees. He has slaves and submissives. Well-paid slaves and submissives, of course. But they don't work for the money. They work for the kink. None of his employees are vanilla."

"Vanilla...that means like straight-laced and normal, right?"

The Mistress smiled at him. "Vanilla means 'not kinky.' It's what we call people outside the scene, the straight types. You, for instance, are vanilla."

"No way. I have more tattoos than Brian Setzer. We counted one day."

"Doesn't matter. It's not clean versus ink, goth versus normal, gay versus straight, Mohawk versus buzz cut. If you don't do kink, you're vanilla. And didn't you just say yourself a few minutes ago up in King's office that you're not one of those guys? Or did I mishear you while I was eavesdropping?"

"I said that, yeah. Just not used to be described as, you know, vanilla." He winced at the word as if she'd called him something really offensive, like "impotent," or "racist," or "a politician."

"Get used to it, Vanilla. If you aren't kinky, that's what you are. There's no shame in being vanilla. Some of my best friends are vanilla."

"Really?" he said with some hope.

"Nope. Come on. Let's get to the club."

Kingsley had a Rolls Royce waiting for them outside his townhouse. The driver hopped out and opened the door for them.

"Nice car," Dante said, studying the interior. "Total pussy wagon."

"You have no idea..." The Mistress said as Dante got comfortable on the bench seat where she'd seen Kingsley fuck at least a dozen different people over the past year. "So tell me about this video. What are you envisioning?"

Dante looked at her and shrugged. Pretty boy. Rock star pretty. Eyeliner, pierced ears, good tan, good smile.

"I don't know. The song's about a guy really in love with this woman, so in love with her he wants to be her slave. You know, all guys feel that way when they fall in love with a woman. They feel..."

"Owned?"

"Yeah. Exactly. Like she could order us to do anything and we'd do it. And in bed, we'd do anything she told us to. It's not kinky. It's just love. All guys feel like that."

The Mistress studied him as street lamps cast their glow through the Rolls window. His face went from dark to light, dark to light, with every lamp they passed.

"Do you ever feel that way when you aren't in love?" She stretched out her leg and rested her booted foot on his thigh. He looked down at her foot but made no attempt to remove or even ask her to take her dirty shoe off his pants.

"What do you mean?" His eyes narrowed at her.

"I mean...do you ever think you'd like to do that, I don't know...every day of your life? Maybe with a woman you weren't in love with. Maybe just a woman you found attractive. Maybe all women."

"I told you, I'm not one of those guys."

"What guys?"

"One of *those* guys. Kinky guys who want to get used by dominatrixes, who want to crawl on their hands and knees for a woman, who want to get ordered around and treated like a fuck toy. That's not me."

"Really? Wonder why you have an erection just talking about it then..."

Dante glanced down at his lap and laughed. "I don't. You can't even—"

"You looked down to see if I could see it through your pants. If you weren't hard right now, you wouldn't have needed to look."

"Maybe I'm just..." He paused mid-sentence to take her leg by the ankle and move her foot back onto the floorboard. "...turned on because I'm in a fucking Rolls Royce with a beautiful woman with black hair and amazing tits in a leather skirt and corset. I think about any guy on the planet would pop one in this situation, even if he was vanilla."

"Which you are, right?" She batted her eyelashes at him.

"Yeah. Right. I'm...vanilla."

"Don't feel bad. Happens to the best of us. Anyway, the club we're going to is called The 8th Circle. It'll give you a boner, too, but don't get excited. You can't film there. King has a couple other smaller kink clubs that you can use for a location shoot if you want. But The 8th Circle's off-limits. It's his baby."

"Why are we going there then?"

"Because that's where my dungeon is. It's where I see my clients. Thought you'd be interested. Aren't you?"

"Why would I want to see your dungeon?" He shifted in his seat.

"Research for your video, of course."

"Yeah, of course. Research."

On the way to the club, Dante asked her a few questions about her background.

D: *How did she become a dominatrix?*
M: Created by God. Trained by Kingsley.

D: *Is it hard being a dominatrix?*
M: More wet than hard.

D: *Is it fun?*
M: Define "fun."

D: *What's the craziest thing you've done as a dominatrix?*
M: I can't answer that without an attorney present.

D: *Do you ever have sex with your clients?*

M: No.

At "no," she saw a flash of disappointment cross his face. Why? Why would he be disappointed she didn't have sex with her clients? Did he consider himself a client because he'd bought two hours of her time to take a stroll through Hell?

Technically, he was. He'd paid for a kinky service and she'd agreed to provide it. Not that she wanted to have sex with him. He was a gorgeous kid with probably enough talent to earn that attitude of his, but nothing about him made her want to jump in bed with him.

No...she had no desire to fuck him. There was no challenge in it. If she came onto him this second, they'd be fucking in five minutes. Fuck fucking. She wanted to get this bad boy to admit he was a sub. She could see it in his eyes that watched her for her pleasure and approval, read it in his body language—passive but alert, eager to please. And yes, aroused...so aroused from merely being in her leather-clad, thigh-high boot-wearing presence.

"Ask me another question," she ordered.

"What's the hardest part about being a dominatrix?"

A good question, she had to give him that. And a thoughtful question. She liked thoughtful. Maybe there was more to this guy than a pretty face, tattoos, and an uncomfortable erection.

"The hardest part...I'm not going to make the obvious penis joke I could make. I'm not. I just made it in my head but I'm not going to say it out loud."

"I appreciate that."

"Seriously, the hardest part is caring about my clients. I try not to care about them because my job gets a lot harder when I do."

"Why?"

Sighing heavily, she leaned back in the seat, stretched out her legs and rested them on the seat next to his thigh.

"I have some fucked-up clients, and I say that with affection. These guys...they have fetishes like you can't believe. They want to drink urine. They can only get off if you beat their cocks with belts. They need me to put puppy ears on them and make them drink out of the dungeon toilet like a dog. I don't care. It doesn't bother me, doesn't freak me out, doesn't gross me out. They're fetishists and that's fine. Takes all kinds. Sex is weird and wonderful and these guys are harmless. They love their wives, their kids. But they have this deep itch inside them that only coming to me can scratch."

"That's pretty crazy. Drink urine?"

Now it was her turn to wag her finger at him.

"Don't judge, Little Grasshopper. Some of

these men could break you in half. They're strong, smart, complicated. That's the thing. They're not boring enough to be vanilla. Most of the men in this country, they're meat-and-pota-toes when it comes to sexuality. Gay or straight, they like it plain and simple. Penetration, thrust, orgasm, sleep. That's it. But then you have my clients. These are the guys who crave escargot, shark fin soup, boiled duck embryos, fucking blowfish. Exotic fare. Those are my people. You eat crazy shit like that and people call you a foodie. You want exotic fare in the bedroom, though, and people call you a sick freak. These men cut their chest open and show me where they keep their souls. It's heartbreaking to care about them. So I don't."

She heard the tenor of her voice changing and she coughed to clear her throat. She didn't care about her clients. Not any of them. They were paychecks and nothing more.

"You do care about them," he said, pressing her.

"You're a Backstreet Boy. What do you know?"

He laughed then, and she had to laugh too.

"I think you and I are both full of shit," she said.

"We are. You respect your clients."

It wasn't a question. She answered it anyway. "I do respect them. It's the scariest thing you can do—walk into a room where you know you're going to meet your real self. Would you do that? If there was a mirror out there and you knew if you looked into it, you'd see the real you...would you look?"

"I think I'd cover that mirror with a sheet and then smash it with a sledgehammer."

"Exactly. Me too. But these guys, they look. So yes, I respect them, I care about them, and I give them what they want and what they need. Then after an hour or two, I send them back out into the world that thinks they're sick perverts. In my dungeon I can protect them, I can make them feel safe and even normal. But out there..." she pointed at the world outside the Rolls Royce's window, "they're on their own."

"You can't save everybody."

"I can't save anybody." She gave him a half-hearted smile. "But it doesn't matter. That's not what they pay me for."

The Rolls brought them to a gray door in a gray parking garage. Dante didn't seem impressed. That was okay. No one was ever impressed by The 8th Circle until they were inside it.

"This is it?" he asked as the driver opened the door for them.

"This is it," she said, pulling her key-ring out and letting him into the front hallway. "But don't be misled. The 8th Circle is like the ugly chick

THE CASE OF THE RELUCTANT ROCK STAR / 89

you take home from the bar at last call because you struck out with everyone else. Then you get her home, drop your pants, and discover she gives the world's best blowjobs."

"I like her already."

"All I'm saying is don't judge the joint by appearances. Oh, watch out," she said, grabbing his arm to steer him from a stain on the floor. "You almost stepped in cum."

He started to look back over his shoulder but no one really needed to see that. With her hand on his arm, she led him down the dimly-lit hallway to a door inside the coat-check booth.

"This is the shortcut to the dungeons," she explained as they took a narrow staircase down. "Otherwise, we'd have to take the elevator to the main club floor. Big crowd tonight. Lots of people playing. You'd definitely get recognized."

"Glad we skipped that part then. I'm trying to be a little anonymous here."

"Hence the guyliner, the sleeveless shirt showing off all your tattoos, the professionally messed-up hair, and the boots that probably cost more than my mortgage payment?"

"You don't let me get away with anything, do you?"

"No."

"Wanna tell me why?" They reached the bottom of the stairs. He leaned back against the wall and crossed his arms over his chest. For a single, beautiful second she saw the real Dante underneath the rock star uniform and the eye-liner and the well-cultivated tan. She saw the man, the musician who cared about his work, his art, and who put on the stupid clothes and the attitude because the world expected it of him. And in that split-second she decided she might like him.

"Because the rest of the world lets you get away with murder. Don't deny it. If you committed an actual murder, would you spend the rest of your life in prison? Or would your handlers cover it up, buy you the best attorneys, and get you off scot-free?"

"I'm not a murderer. I'm a nice guy."

"I don't care how nice you are. No matter how nice you are, you can't be as nice to the world as the world's been nice to you. How much money are you worth?"

"That's kind of a personal question."

"You asked me if I have sex with my clients, but me asking you your net worth is a personal question?"

"Point taken. I'm at about 97 million at the last audit."

"Good. Now are you 97 million dollars worth of nice to the world?"

He shook his head and shrugged. "I don't know if anyone could be that nice. That's a lotta nice."

"You really need 97 million to get through the night? How much does your fucking hair gel cost?"

He laughed out loud then and ran his fingers through his hair. "It's pricy shit."

"Wonder what brand of hair gel that homeless guy in the parking garage uses?"

"You're giving me shit because I haven't given all my money to the homeless?"

The Mistress took a step toward him and stared him right into his hazel eyes. He started to glance away but she took him by the chin and forced him to meet her gaze.

"I'm giving you shit because no one else in this wide world would dare to," she said. "Right?"

Slowly he nodded his agreement. "I can't help it," he said, raising his hands in surrender. "You get to the level of fame and money I'm at, and you're surrounded by nothing but Yes Men."

"That's why women like me exist." She flicked the end of his nose hard enough he flinched. "We're the antidote to Yes Men. Come on. I'll show you my dungeon. You'll like it."

She dragged him by his shirt collar down the hall.

"Hey, this shirt was expensive," he protested at her rough treatment.

"So is my time. You don't hear me bitching, do you?"

At the end of the hallway she stopped in front of her dungeon door and pulled out a key.

"We're all mad here?" Dante said, reading the words on the door.

"Cheshire Cat," she explained. *"Alice in Wonderland.* You should read it. It's trippy as fuck. Better than LSD."

"I don't do drugs." She heard a note of pride in his voice.

"I'll get you a medal. Now...welcome to my Wonderland." Throwing open the door, she took a step back and let Dante in first. Newbies to the dungeon were usually a little surprised at the sight that greeted them. Dante was no different.

"This doesn't look like a dungeon. It looks like a bedroom. A nice bedroom." He nodded his approval at the king-size, four-poster bed, layered in red and gold brocade sheets and pillows, the oil lamps, the erotic art on the walls. "No whips and chains?"

"Plenty of whips and chains. That's behind door number two." She led him past the bed and into the second room of her suite.

His eyes went wide as dinner plates as he took in the view. "Fuck."

"I don't fuck on the clock," she said, giving him a sly wink. "That's a St. Andrew's Cross. I put people on there to flog and whip them. Among other things. I've got the hospital bed over there for my medical fetishists. That's a rack. The throne is a lot of fun for bondage."

"That's a coffin, right?" Dante pointed to the far wall.

"Yeah, I have some clients into sensory deprivation. I don't even think it's sexual for those guys. I think they just want to be left alone. Anyway, they come in, I put them in the coffin, I sit and read a book. They get out an hour or two later, happy as clams. Easiest grand you could ever make."

"Nice. I don't get the pain thing. I mean, I'm covered in tattoos but they hurt like hell and no part of me was turned on during the process."

"Well, you're not a masochist. People like pain for a lot of reasons. I have clients who suffer from chronic pain, and getting a good full-body flogging helps their body produce more adrenaline and other pain-fighting hormones. I have some clients who can't get aroused unless you hurt them first. One's a cop. One's a doctor. Takes all kinds."

"I guess so. I mean, it makes sense. I know some musicians who really can't perform unless they're on drugs. They need the rush."

"I'm a lot easier on the body than coke. Not all my clients are into pain, though." She turned off the lights in the dungeon and returned to the bedroom. "I have some male subs who are nothing but subs. They just want to take orders from a woman. They come here and worship my feet and fetch things for me and masturbate for me."

"So you can be kinky and not like pain?"

"Oh yeah, I know a lot of female subs especially who love submitting but don't like to be hurt. Their masters or mistresses will tell them to go suck some stranger's cock and you'll think they just won the lottery. You get a flogger near them and they curl up in the fetal position and cry."

"Weird. I thought all kink was, you know, the whips and chains."

She shook her head. "This world is much bigger than that."

"Hmm..." He crossed his arms over his chest and leaned back against the bedpost. "Maybe I am kinky."

She raised her eyebrow at him as she sat in a large, ornate chair and threw her leg over the arms. "Do tell."

"I...it's kind of weird." He grimaced. "You probably wouldn't believe me if I told you."

"I lost my virginity to a Catholic priest, and that's one of my least weird sexual encounters. Trust me, I'll believe you."

His eyes went wide again, and she could only smile. She loved shocking the newbies.

"Okay...here's the story, and it's all true. It's

gonna sound like something out of *Penthouse Letters*. But it happened."

"Try me." With all the wild sex that surrounded her on a daily basis, his story would have to involve alien anal probes to get her to question his soliloquy.

"I learned to play guitar pretty young. Natural musician. Guitar and piano. Bass too. I was really shy, though, so I didn't play much outside of the house. My older sister, Cate, she was super popular. Like no one in our high school even knew we were related because I hid in the background so much and stayed quiet. Cate had these three friends—Polly, Amie, and Mona. They'd been best friends since they started high school. They were their own clique."

"Pretty girls?"

"Gorgeous. And nice too, believe it or not. Nice to me. Cate and I got along great at home. Our dad died when we were pretty young and Mom dated a lot. My sister and I sort of stuck together. She was protective of me. And her friends liked me too."

"Oh, this is already getting interesting." The Mistress grinned at him.

"Just wait." He took a ragged breath. "I was a sophomore. Sixteen. Cate and her friends were seniors. Mom was staying over at her new boyfriend's house. Cate had the girls over for a sleepover. She wanted to sneak out and stay with her boyfriend, too, and her friends were helping cover for her. So it was me alone in the house with these gorgeous girls. We got into the liquor cabinet and drank a little. But none of us were drunk. Just buzzed. Happy. Talkative. Amie asked me if I had a girlfriend, if I'd ever had sex before. I don't think I've ever been so embarrassed in my life. But I told her the truth, which was no. The girls all looked at each other...then they looked at me..."

"Why am I hearing porn music in the background?"

"Exactly. So Amie hears that I'm still a virgin, and she leans over the coffee table and kisses me right in front of the two girls. Amie was the ringleader. Wherever she went, the other girls followed. So then Mona kissed me and then Polly. I nearly came in my pants. But it wasn't just kissing. Amie stood up and crooked her finger at me, motioning me to follow her. She brought me to my own bedroom and..."

"Fucked you? I'm guessing she fucked you."

"She fucked me. And it was amazing. Amie was very take-charge. She was all 'kiss my nipples, suck my clit, put your fingers in me...' She liked giving orders and I loved taking them."

"Then what happened?"

"She kissed me goodnight and left the room. I thought that was it. I was just lying in bed naked and smiling at the ceiling and thanking God for inventing women. But then the door opened. Mona's turn. Amie must have told her how well I took orders because she was just as bossy in bed. After that, Polly came in."

"You fucked three girls in a row the night you lost your virginity?"

"I was sixteen. I could have fucked twenty girls that night. Anyway, after that, sleepovers at the house got a lot more interesting. After Cate fell asleep, at least one of them would sneak into my bedroom. The girls had all dated jocks and jerks. And yeah, they ignored me at school, acted like I didn't exist. But it was for the best. I loved being their little secret. Amie told me one night I was the only guy she'd been with who could make her come. I loved going down on them. Loved it."

"Powerful memories."

"Very," he exhaled, his skin flushing with re-membered desire. "The girls...they never called me by name. They always called me Rock Star. 'Hey Rock Star, come play a song for us...' I would have done anything they told me to. Anything."

"Rock Star, that's cute. You loved that they used you like a fuck toy."

"God yes. I don't get that anymore. Backstage the fans, they worship me. The women are too nervous just being around me to give me any kind of order. They lay there in bed like it's some kind of honor to be fucked by me. I remember what it felt like with my sister's friends. I was the nobody they'd deigned to fuck. I loved worshipping their bodies. That's what I was into. Not being worshipped. I get enough of that shit every time I walk out the door."

"So let me get this straight." The Mistress stood up and came over to him. "You love worshipping the female body, being treated like a sex toy to be used for a woman's pleasure, and pleasuring multiple women in one night? You don't want to be worshipped. You want to be treated like an object, a sex slave, a piece of property who exists only to give women pleasure?"

Dante didn't answer at first. He couldn't even seem to look in her eyes. "I fantasize about it a lot. About being with women who own me so much they won't even let me come." His voice dropped to a whisper. "Is that weird?"

"No," she whispered back right into his ear. "It's sexy, it's erotic, and it's so *not* vanilla."

"I always felt weird about it. Unmanly. It's not very manly to want women to...I don't even know the word."

"Top. You feel weird because you want women to top you. And there's nothing unmanly about giving a woman orgasms and putting her pleasure before yours. Nothing wrong with being a male sub. You don't have to be a chest-thumping alpha to find the clit."

"Trust me, I know where the clit is."

"Now that *is* the sort of thing that would win you a medal down here. Want your medal?"

"Yeah," he said, laughing. "Sure. I'd love a medal."

"Are you STD-free?"

"Um, yes. Had to get a full physical two weeks ago for insurance for the new tour. Got tested for everything."

"Do you have a girlfriend?"

"No. We broke up two months ago. She was just another Yes Man."

"Good. Go wash your face. Get rid of the eyeliner. Take off the rock star boots and for fuck's sake, comb your hair like a normal person. No more costumes. I want to see the real you. Bathroom's over there. I need to make a phone call."

* * *

When he came out of the bathroom, Dante looked like the handsome, nice, sweet male submissive she knew lurked underneath all that eye makeup and hair gel.

"There's our girls," she said when she heard a tentative knock on the dungeon door. "You stand there. I'll get this."

"What is this?" he asked, looked humble and nervous, and surprisingly young.

"Turns out I'm all out of medals. I got you this instead."

She opened the door and ushered two lovely young women inside. One was a tall beauty with tattoos and rainbow-striped hair. The other was pale and petite, with lustrous brown hair that fell halfway down her back in soft waves.

"Simone, Cassie, this is my friend—"

"Devon," he said. "My name's Devon."

The Mistress raised an eyebrow, but he ignored her. Either he was trying to be incognito, or he'd finally become comfortable enough to let his real name slip.

"Ladies, 'Devon' is a new friend of mine. A submissive. He's looking to explore some of his fantasies. One of them involves being used as a fuck toy. A little birdie told me that Devon here loves giving women orgasms. He'd rather give orgasms than have them himself. Isn't that nice?"

"I love male subs," Cassie signed, leaning her head on Simone's shoulder.

"They really are handy to have around." Simone kissed Cassie on the top of the head.

The Mistress gestured at the bed. "Well...shall we?"

Cassie looked Dante up and down. "He's gorgeous."

"He really is. Looks familiar too. You come to the club before?" Simone asked.

"No. I just...I have that kind of face."

"Girls..." The Mistress clapped her hands. "Condoms in the drawer. He's all yours. I'll be over here supervising. Let me know if I can assist."

Cassie and Simone came up to Dante and kissed him on the lips, one by one. As Cassie deepened the kiss, Simone raised his arms over his head and pulled his shirt off. Simone ran her hands all over his back and shoulders while Cassie brought his hands to her breasts. The two women pulled him gently to the bed and laid him on his back. The girls were submissives, both of them. But they loved sex, they loved men, and they loved submitting to her. Being on The Mistress's good side meant being invited into Kingsley's inner sanctum. And right now both girls were definitely on The Mistress's good side.

Simone slid off the bed and stripped off all her clothes apart from her elaborately-laced high heels. She sat with her back to the headboard of the bed and spread her legs wide.

"Fingers first," she said to Dante and he seemed to have no problem taking that sort of order. Cassie took off her clothes while Dante slipped two and then three fingers into Simone. Whatever he was doing seemed to be working because in less than a minute, Simone the submissive gave an unmistakable order. "Tongue now."

Simone spread her folds and gave Dante better access to her clitoris. He'd said he loved going down on women, and he certainly showed incredible enthusiasm for the task.

Cassie crawled back onto the bed and began caressing Simone's breasts, teasing her pierced nipples while Dante lapped at her vagina, sucked on her clitoris. All Simone could do was grab the bars of the headboard and moan and moan until an orgasm seized her with body-wracking force.

"Wow..." With that one word Simone collapsed tiredly onto the bed. "Your turn, Cass."

"You don't have to tell me twice," Cassie said as she pushed Dante onto his back. The Mistress wondered if this was like his first time with Amie. On his back, nervous, aroused beyond comprehension, wondering what the hell he was doing while a beautiful older girl touched parts of his body no one but he had touched before. She had to wonder where that trio of girls were now. Beautiful, erotic, and loved giving sexual orders to men? They sounded like perfect additions to The 8th Circle. Kingsley was always looking for a few good dommes.

Cassie brought Dante's mouth to her breasts and he latched onto a nipple. He caressed her other breast while she straddled his lap and ground her hips against his. Once Simone recovered enough from her orgasm to see straight again, she did Dante the favor of opening his jeans and freeing his erection. Simone took a condom out of the nightstand and rolled it onto him.

Dante stretched out onto his back as Cassie took him into her hand and guided him inside her. With her hands on his broad, tattooed chest, she rode him with long oval undulations of her hips.

"I know it feels good," The Mistress said to Dante from her chair near the bed, "but don't forget, no coming. Just the girls, not you."

"I promise I won't. As long as she comes, that's all that matters."

"Oh, she's coming," Cassie said as she bucked her hips harder against him, using him like nothing more than a dildo that just so happened to be attached to a human body. Dante cupped Cassie's breasts as she moved on him, teasing her nipples until they were bright red and swollen. "She is definitely coming."

"Take your time," Dante said from underneath her. "I can stay here all day..."

He moved one hand between their bodies and found her clitoris. He pressed up against the tight bud and Cassie gasped. She'd promised she was coming and she hadn't been lying. With a cry they probably heard in the dungeon at the end of the hall, Cassie climaxed on top of him.

She rolled onto her back and lay there panting. Pointing from Simone to Dante, Cassie rasped, "Go get him."

Simone required no more encouragement. "Did you come?" she asked as she straddled Dante's chest and sat on his stomach.

"No."

"He doesn't have permission to come," The Mistress chimed in from her chair. She should have brought her book with her to work on while the kids played. She'd remember that for the next gangbang. "He hasn't earned it yet."

"You heard the lady," Dante said, smiling up at Simone.

"Good. I want to fuck you too. Now."

"Yes, Ma'am."

Even from her corner of the room, The Mistress could hear the happiness in his voice. Not pleasure. Not desire. Happiness. Being used by women made him happy. And the ladies weren't complaining either.

Simone stripped him of the rest of his clothes. "Can we tie him down, Mistress?" she asked, fishing a new condom out of the box.

"Not this time. He's a newbie. Gotta save something for the sequel," she said. She and Dante hadn't discussed his feelings about bondage.

"Oh, fine." Simone sounded playfully disappointed. "Cassie can hold him down then. That okay, Devon?"

"You won't hear me objecting."

"Good boy." Simone gave him a patronizing couple of slaps on the cheek like a proud Italian grandmother. Looked like Simone might have a bit of a switch-side to her.

She pushed him into her and started riding him while Cassie held him by his wrists, pressing him into the bed. As strong as he was, he could have easily escaped the clutches of the girls, but The Mistress had a feeling that getting away hadn't even crossed his mind. After a minute, Simone pulled off him, turned around and started to ride him reverse-cowgirl.

"Do you actually enjoy that?" The Mistress asked. "That is my least favorite position. I feel like the cock's poking my damn ribcage."

"It's kind of weird," Simone admitted. "But he's a good size for this position. Not too big, not too small. You have to tilt just right or it does hit the wrong spots."

"Are you enjoying it?" The Mistress asked Dante. A trick question.

"Doesn't matter," he said. "As long as she is."

"Spoken like a true sub." The Mistress beamed with pride.

While Simone continued riding him, Cassie swung around and straddled his head. Now he had his cock buried in Simone and his tongue buried in Cassie. If he died underneath those two women, he would, at the very least, die a happy man.

Whatever that magic tongue of his was doing to Cassie certainly seemed to make her a happy woman. And Simone wasn't complaining either as her hips pumped against him.

"Ladies?" The Mistress interjected. "Not to interrupt, but he's not going to be able to warn you he's about to come if his tongue is three inches inside Cassie."

Cassie sighed heavily as she moved off Dante's face. "I guess you're right, Mistress. I'll wait my turn."

"Oh, sit on his face all you want," The Mistress said. "He just needs a ducky. Bottom drawer."

"Ducky?" Dante said, panting as Simone kept moving on him.

Cassie dug in the second nightstand drawer and pulled out a squeaky toy duck.

"Ducky," Cassie said, putting it into Dante's hand. "Squeeze it if you're getting too close. That way I know to get off. I mean, get off you."

"I'm holding a squeaky toy duck in a dungeon while two women fuck me and a dominatrix supervises..." Dante said as he stared at the ducky in his hand. "This is not how I imagined my day ending."

"Really?" The Mistress asked. "It's exactly

how I imagined my day ending. Carry on."

Cassie sat astride Dante's face again. He went back to work on her with gusto and with gusto she came a few minutes later. Right after her orgasm, he squeaked the duck in a warning. Simone sighed and dismounted from him.

Dante lay on the bed as he breathed through his nose, no doubt trying to settle his arousal.

"Simone's not going to get herself off," The Mistress reminded him. "Someone's got to do it for her."

"I volunteer." He raised his hand in the air and the girls giggled. "Suggestions?"

"She likes fingers. Oh, even better." The Mistress disappeared into her dungeon and returned with a vibrator. "Sanitized and fully charged. Go get her."

Simone threw her legs wide open and Dante teased her with the vibrator while Cassie watched and assisted. When done, Cassie expressed an interest in some double penetration. Dante lubed her up and penetrated her anally while Simone pushed a condom-covered vibrator gently into her vagina.

An hour passed as Dante took turns bringing each woman to orgasm...with his hands, his mouth, his cock, and then back through the gamut again. By the time each of them had come three times, they were all exhausted, sweating, and barely mobile.

The Mistress gave the three of them a round of applause and promptly kicked Cassie and Simone out of the room. With much grumbling and complaining, they put on their clothes and kissed Dante—aka "Devon"—goodbye. Of the three, he alone had not come during the sex. He remained rock hard and smiling.

Once alone again, The Mistress sat back down on her throne and beckoned Dante to kneel at her feel. Naked and aroused, he did as told.

"You had fun being a fuck toy today," she said.

"That's the best sex I've had since high school."

The Mistress tapped her chin. "Now that's a sentence you don't hear very often."

"I've had a lot of bad sex since high school."

"Was it bad or was it just not what you wanted?"

"Not what I wanted. But tonight, with them? Oh my God...that was perfect."

"We can do it again sometime. Maybe work some bondage in. Make you into a real sex slave. Get a real domme in here to do you. How does that sound?"

"I think I'd like that, Mistress."

"Would you like to come for me?"

"Yes...so much. Please."

"Come for me then. Wait...no. Say please

again."

Dante looked at her with humble beseeching eyes. "Please...please, Mistress."

"Okay, go for it."

He stroked himself while she watched with a raised eyebrow, daring him to impress her. Closing his eyes, he moved his hand faster on himself as his breathing grew more ragged. A minute passed...another...

"Having trouble there, Cock Star?" The Mistress asked him.

He kept stroking but without coming. "I've never done this in front of somebody before."

The Mistress rolled her eyes. "'Head Like a Hole,'" she said.

Dante's eyes popped wide open. "What?"

"My favorite Nine Inch Nails song," she confessed with a wink.

Dante came in seconds. She handed him a moist towelette, noticed the amount of semen that had landed on her rug, and handed him two more.

"You do know Trent Reznor," he said as he cleaned himself up, a broad smile on his face.

"Of course. I'm a child of the nineties." She extended her leg so that her foot hung in the air two inches from his lips. He kissed her boot reverently. "Eddie Vedder and my right hand gave me my first orgasm."

"Mistress...I think I'm in love with you." He

kissed his way from her toes to her knee.

"Well," she sighed, "you're only human."

* * *

So I was right about Cock Star. First of all, there was no video shoot. Total ruse. Dante—who swears that's his real name, and that "Devon" was something he only uses at hotels—had been dying for years to explore kink. He'd never felt safe or comfortable enough to come to us as a client or seeker. Hence the "video shoot" cover story.

Thankfully, he's feeling better about his desires now. I see him once a month, and Cassie and Simone see him every chance they get. They might be submissives but even they can get on board with a male sub that wants nothing more than to give them as many orgasms as humanly possible.

He's turning into a fantastic male submissive. I have two dommes banging down my door to collar him. But I think I'll keep him to myself a little while longer. Needs more training. Plus he's rich as fuck and leaves amazing tips (including concert tickets).

Speaking of concerts, I went to his most recent show at Madison Square Garden. Pretty good music. (The Black Sheets are no Pearl Jam, just for the record.) He debuted a new song at the show. It's called "Bootkisser," and contains the lyric "I'd rather kiss your boot than let them kiss my ass."

Wonder where he got the inspiration…

FILE #4

Client Name: CONFIDENTIAL — White male (age 44)

Profession: I'm not even going to justify this question with an answer

Inclination: Switch

Level of Experience: Whatever is one level higher than "has done every kind of kink ever invented"

Orientation: Bisexual

* * *

So...let me tell you a little about him—

No, not yet. I can't start with him yet. Let me tell you about *me* first.

As a dominatrix, you never know whose ass you're going to kick today. It might be an eighty-year-old foot fetishist who wants to get in one last good rub before kicking off to that big shoe rack in the sky. It might be the CEO of a Fortune 500 company who needs punished for all the naughty things he did to his employees' pension fund that week. It might be some sweet kid, barely eighteen, who pretends to be all nice and normal and vanilla with his friends when they ogle the girls at strip clubs, but at night boots up the fetish porn and jerks off to pictures of women in eight-inch stilettos walking on the backs of bound and gagged men with leashes around their scrotums. He doesn't know what he is, but he knows I can show him.

The fetishist, the freak, the fearful...I love them all. I'm one of them so I know how they feel, I know what they need, and I want nothing more than to give it to them. For a price, of course. In this world, money imparts value. The only way to cheapen the sacred acts I perform would be to give them away for free. I see all kinds and I do all things and I get paid well for it. Yet even with this endless revolving door of precious perverts, I get a surprise every now and then.

Because sometimes, when I least expect it, he walks in. He is special, this client. With all my other clients, it's work, it's a job. Sometimes a fun job.

Sometimes I think I'd rather be sitting in a cubicle with office drones than doing what I'm doing. But with him, it's not a job. It's not professional. With him, it's personal. And because it's personal, it's draining, exhausting...it uses me up so I have nothing left to give for a day or two. I charge him more because of that, and he pays willingly. But for this special client, I make sure he gets his money's worth. Why? Because we're the same, me and him, not that either of us would ever admit that to anyone else. We're both switches. If you don't know what a switch is, allow me to enlighten you. Switches are submissives. We're also dominants. Often we're also both sadists and masochists, masters and slaves. We're distrusted in the kink community. Dominants are afraid to have switches as their subs. After all, she might decide halfway through a scene it's her turn to start doing the flogging. Think about the bullshit they say about bisexual people. *If you were a straight woman, would you want to date a bisexual man? If you did, wouldn't you have a nagging gnawing question in the back of your mind—is he really gay and just hiding behind me?* Switches get that garbage from both sides. The doms think we're weak. The subs think we're indecisive sluts who want to get it from everybody (they're only half right).

That's okay. We understand each other. That's why he, my most special client, comes to me and no one else.

The Mistress wouldn't say he was her favorite client, not to his face anyway. When he showed up, she knew he would be the last person she saw that day. He took more out of her than any of the other men who came to her dungeon at the club. He took the most time, the most effort, and he never made an appointment.

Two weeks ago, he came to her dungeon. It had been about two months since their previous session together. It might have taken three weeks for him to heal completely from it. She'd worked him over thoroughly that night, just the way he liked it. The other nine weeks between that night and this one, he'd been too busy to see her, or simply not in the mood to be destroyed. The mood struck him at the oddest times and for seemingly no reason. She never asked him the reasons why he decided to show up at her feet.

He wasn't there to talk. He wanted pain, and The Mistress wanted to give it to him.

On a Wednesday afternoon at about four, he strolled into her suite without knocking. The Mistress lay stretched out on the bed reading a book. *Of Human Bondage* by W. Somerset Maugham. A disappointing book. Well-written but she was two hundred pages in, and no one had even been tied up yet. She looked up from her book as he swept in the door, shutting and locking it behind him. He did this often, came into her dungeon. He had every right to. But locking the door meant only one thing.

Play-time.

She didn't speak. She shut the book and tossed it onto the nightstand. From the small table she pulled an elegant black mask that covered only the top half of the face. Like the good and well-trained submissive he was playing that day, he kept his eyes on the floor as she approached him. In all the world, she'd only ever met one man she found more attractive than the one standing before her. Night and day, he and the other man were. The submissive masochist in front of her had olive skin, dark eyes, dark as a sin-stained soul, and black hair with a slight roguish wave that fell to right above his shoulders. And at the moment, he had on far too much clothing.

"Lose the shoes. Shirt, too," she ordered as

she slipped the masquerade mask over his eyes. It had eyeholes—she didn't want to blindfold him, only put him in a mental place where he could become another person...someone other than the one who'd walked in her door and the one who would crawl out of it. Plus, no denying, the man looked fucking hot in the mask. With this particular client, she allowed herself to enjoy her attraction to him.

He shucked off his jacket and she took it from him, tossing it on the floor. The embroidered vest came off next. It too landed on the floor. Then the shirt. Raising her hands to his chest, she caressed his strong broad shoulders, his collarbone, the hollow of his throat. She loved to tease him with pleasure before torturing him with pain. With another client who shared his sort of desires and fetishes, she would have put a collar on him. But no, never with him. He had one hard limit, only one: no collars. He was willing to surrender to a world of pain, but drew the line at such an obvious sign of ownership within the kink community.

That didn't mean she wasn't about to treat him like a dog.

"Stay," she said as she went back to the bedside table. She pulled a thin black rope lead from the drawer and returned to him. God, how he hated the lead. Loathed it. The man had pride.

On his own time, maybe. Not on hers.

She leashed it around his neck and slipped the end of the rope through the hole at the other end. It would tighten around his neck if he resisted her. A choke rope. Holding the end of the lead, she took four steps back to stand three feet from him. She tugged once on the lead and he didn't move. Good. She loved it when he gave her an excuse to punish him. Raising her hand she wrapped the rope one time...two times...three times around her palm. With every turn of her hand, she pulled him closer to her.

"I know you hate this," she said.

"You know me well, Maîtresse."

She yanked him to her so they were eye-to-eye. She wore eight-inch platform stiletto boots that day, otherwise she would have been staring down the center of his chest. Not a bad place to stare. He had a beautiful body, no denying that. Lean and muscular. Riddled with old scars. She wouldn't add any to his vast collection today. Only cuts, welts, and bruises. All injuries that would heal quickly. If he wanted scars, he'd have to pay extra and make an appointment.

"I do know you...but not well enough," she said. "I think I want to get to know you better today. Let's go into my office. Come along."

She gave the rope another yank and led him into the second room of her suite. The front room was the bedroom, which she rarely used with clients. Sexual favors were granted for female clients and lovers only—not male clients. But the second room, the dungeon, housed all her toys. Including her most favorite toy of all.

"Do you know anything about the story of St. Andrew?" she asked as she dragged him by the lead to the ten-foot tall, X-shaped St. Andrew's Cross at the back of the room.

"I'm vaguely familiar with him."

She removed the lead and tossed it aside. "Up," she ordered and he stepped in front of the cross. "Arms."

He knew the drill well enough she didn't even have to give him the orders. She didn't have to, but she wanted to. She wanted to and he wanted her to. To be brutalized and dominated— that's what he came for. To be dominated and brutalized—that's why he came.

But he wasn't allowed to come yet. He had to earn it first.

She locked his wrists to the bars of the cross and left him standing strung up while she went to a tiny box and pulled out five silver needle-sharp fingernail extenders. Talons, she called them. How fortuitous that she'd gotten a brand-new set of them this week and sanitized them with fire that very morning.

"So, St. Andrew," she said. "Fun guy. He was Peter's brother, supposedly. *The* Peter—the first pope. They were fishermen, both of them. Brutal profession, catching fish. The rope nets tore up the hands. The work was backbreaking. And imagine how the fish felt—caught in a net, dragged to the surface, drowning in air. They couldn't get free no matter how hard they struggled."

He pulled on the bounds that held him to the cross. "I can sympathize," he said, the lightest hint of amusement in his voice.

"And worse than the net was, of course, the hook."

With those words she pricked his back with her talons. He flinched and five tiny drops of blood appeared on his shoulder like a red constellation.

"That fucking hook," she sighed. "Can you imagine how much it would hurt to have a hook in your mouth? And then to get dragged by that hook all the way to the surface...brutal."

She moved her hand down, and left another five bleeding pinholes in his back.

"We are solitary, poor, nasty, brutish creatures, we humans," he said between winces. "We deserve all the punishment God has to give us."

"I suppose that makes me an instrument of God's wrath, doesn't it? I kind of like the thought of that. Here's a little more wrath for you."

She ran her talons in a straight line down his back, leaving four shallow bleeding rivulets about three inches long. He panted through the pain and she could only smile. With her free hand, she reached around his hip and felt his erection pressing against her hand. Nasty and brutish—his favorite way to play. Luckily, it was hers too.

"Poor St. Andrew…he was crucified too. An X-shaped cross, not T-shaped. He didn't think he was worthy to die on the same sort of cross as his Lord. His brother Peter had already been crucified upside-down. He couldn't go that route either. They got very creative with their crucifying. We might have to get creative one of these days…"

The Mistress let that threat hang in the air as she unbuttoned his trousers. While she stroked him with one hand, her other hand continued to prick his back with tiny pinholes. She'd undergone this particular torture herself a time or two. Bee stings hurt worse but only barely. And at least the bee died after stinging you. No such luck with a sadistic Mistress. She wasn't going anywhere and had nothing but more pain to give him.

"I've always wondered about your love of pain." She ran a finger from the base of his erection to the tip and back down again. "Born masochist? Or made? Nature? Nurture?"

"Who knows? I didn't know I loved it until someone hurt me the first time. After that I couldn't get enough. Was I made? *Peut-être?* Then again, I didn't know I loved Cabernet Sauvignon until I had my first glass either. But the taste buds, they were already there..."

"I suppose it doesn't matter how you got it. It's here. Drink up." At that, she stroked him hard as she left four more parallel lines of blood on his back.

She removed her talons and sat them aside before stripping her victim completely naked. As she dragged his pants down his legs, she bit his upper thigh, lower thigh, and calf hard enough to leave three black bruises. She couldn't help herself—the man did have exquisite legs.

Now that she had his back bared and bleeding, she decided it might be time to give him some real pain. Of course, she'd broken the skin. That meant a few more precautions would be necessary. She opened a case that had a new deerskin flogger in it—never before used. Doing edge-play with a client meant more work for her during and after. Usually, she charged through the nose for even a cut or two. But for him, well, he was a special case. Not that this was a freebie. To quote The Boss: *No freebies. Ever.*

She stood behind him and examined her handiwork. "You're bleeding," she said. "A lot."

"Merci," was his sole response, the only one she expected, the only one she wanted.

"But they're tiny little cuts. If I left them

alone, they'd heal up in two days. Where's the fun in that?"

She raised the flogger and brought it down hard onto his bleeding back. She struck again. And again. She struck high and hard, low and deep. She added welts to the cuts, bruises to the welts. The tips of the flogger tails smeared the blood and soon his entire back had turned a rusty red.

After a good (for her) half-hour of flogging, she dropped the deerskin and let him catch his breath.

"Have you ever safed out with anyone?" she asked as she came to stand at his side again. A few drops of semen had leaked from his cock and she caught them on her fingertip.

"*Non,* Maîtresse."

"You like pain that much? Or is it pride?"

"You know the answer to that already. Why did you never safe out with him?"

"I did," she corrected him. "But only once."

"Why?"

"Because," she said as she wrapped her hand around his erection again and squeezed to the point of pain. "He ordered me to marry him."

"He must be a masochist too," he said through gritted teeth.

The Mistress could only laugh. "Oh, you're gonna get it big time for that."

Big time meant the cane. Not the rattan cane

she used to leave the hand-sized bruises on a client's ass or thighs. No, what she needed was the little cane—white plastic, long as a conductor's baton. In fact, it had always reminded her of a baton, one she used to conduct a symphony of pain.

She started under his left shoulder-blade and left a two-inch raised welt by flicking the baton against his skin. An unassuming little toy, no one ever dreamed it hurt as much as it did, not until they felt the fiery force of it. Getting cut with a razor hurt less than this little devil.

"Breathe," she instructed as she flicked it against him again, barely half an inch below the first welt. "Don't forget to breathe..."

"I'm breathing," he said, although she'd seen him holding his breath seconds earlier. He'd passed out in their sessions, usually during breath-play scenes. No harm, no foul. Fainting, falling, crying, wailing, being hauled to your breaking point and left there staring into the abyss—that's what happened behind locked dungeon doors when the vanilla world wasn't watching and the monsters came out to play. In this room with this man, she had no one to answer to but God, and God wasn't asking any questions right now.

"Good boy. You pass out on me and it's game over. We don't want that, do we? You haven't even come yet. You take thirty more of these," she said, flicking him once more and smiling at the searing red line on his back, "and we'll discuss throwing a little pleasure into this mix."

"Thirty-three welts?"

"What? I like my biblical numbers. Now shut up and breathe." She flicked him again, working her way down his entire left side. By the time she was done with him, there would be no part of his body from his neck to his hip that wasn't either bruised, bleeding, or scoured with welts. He loved his souvenirs, as he called them. Souvenirs from his holidays in Hell.

Up his right side, she decorated him with more welts. To add a little challenge, she made him count the flicks of her baton for the last seventeen strikes.

His "one" sounded strong. The "five" sounded pained. By "ten," he gasped the number. At "thirteen," she could barely hear him.

By seventeen, she'd broken him. It took almost a full minute to get him to say the number.

"I'm waiting..." She ran the baton over his back, letting it tickle his savaged skin. "You want a little pleasure, don't you? If you want a break from the pain, you have to say the number. You know I'll let you hang here all night until you say it. I'll get my book and pull up a chair and read. I have all the time in the world..."

He swallowed hard and shuddered. Poor dear. She'd piled on the pain today on only one part of his body—his back. Usually that much pain she'd spread out over a larger area—back, ass, thighs... Those sorts of niceties she reserved for other clients, however. Gentler clients, weaker clients, tamer clients. But this client got her best because he paid for her best. And when someone paid for her best, she did her worst.

"It's only one more...you can take one more, can't you?"

His only reply was a nod. She saw that behind the mask, he'd closed his eyes, and she took the opportunity to simply take him in.

Who was he? She'd asked herself that question since the day she'd met him when she'd only been sixteen years old. What secrets did he keep behind those eyes and inside that scarred and beautiful body of his? She could have beaten the secrets out of him, but she knew him well enough to know that, in fact, she didn't want to know every one of his secrets.

"Seventeen," he said in a clear voice, raising up his head.

The seventeenth flick of the baton was the hardest by far. "That was for the 'He must be a masochist' crack."

She kissed his welt before dropping the baton on the floor and breaking it with her foot. She never used a toy on anyone else after she'd used it on him. It was the lone sign of respect she afforded him when he was in submission to her.

Once a flogger or cane or blade touched his body, it would never touch another. She either broke it or set it aside to be used in the future on him and only him.

"I deserved that." He relaxed in the bonds, resting his head against his upper arm.

"You did. And worse. I'm trying to decide how much worse."

"I will submit to anything you desire, Maîtresse."

"I know you will. That's the problem. Too many choices. I could cane your legs. I could pour some scalding candle-wax on your testicles. Hmm...So many ways to make you my bitch. Hard to choose just one."

"Are you open to suggestion, Maîtresse?"

He turned his head and peered at her through the space between his arm and the cross. Of course, they both knew he shouldn't be making eye contact with her. This evening, she was in charge, she was the dominant, and he was nothing but property for her to use and abuse any way she wanted. But she had trouble being angry at him for something as human as looking in her eyes. How would she see his hunger, his need, his humble desperation if she didn't see his eyes? She'd give him a pass on the eye contact this time. She'd only flog him a little more. Nothing vicious. She'd save the viciousness for the next time he did it.

"And what, pray tell, is your suggestion?"

His only answer was to laugh, and the laugh was all she needed to hear. A low, throaty, masculine, insinuating, thigh-melting, knee-shivering, panties-suddenly-disappear-and-end-up-hanging-off-the-bedpost sort of laugh. Glad to know he wasn't the only one in the mood.

"Well, it is a good suggestion."

"*Merci*, Maîtresse."

"If I'm going to do it, you're going to have to earn it."

"I understand," he said, almost solemnly. Nothing like a threat of having to "earn it" could put the fear of God back into a sub. She'd already ripped his back apart in three different ways. Time to give the front side The Mistress treatment.

She unlocked his wrists from the cross and turned him around, slamming his back roughly into the painted wood. He flinched visibly as his back made contact with the cross. He'd be in agony for a week at least after today. Maybe two.

As she buckled his wrists to the cross, she felt his erection pressing against her stomach. Nothing got him harder than pain. Not threesomes, not orgies, not dominating, not submitting, not anything. She knew his need for release was so strong now it had become yet another form of torture. Good.

"You're dying to come, aren't you?" she asked

as she pushed her hip into him, sending him into shudders.

"Death would be a relief right now."

"I won't let you die. That would be too merciful. I'm not really in the mood to be merciful today. I am, however, in the mood to redecorate. You know I love your scars, the bullet wounds, all of them...but I think you could use some new designs here." She ran her hand all over his chest. "Nothing permanent. Wait here." With a light and insulting slap-tap on his cheek, she sauntered off. She returned with a Wartenberg wheel and her violet wand.

"Now I know you don't play with violet wands, and that's fine. But I do. And the reason I do is because they can make such wonderful patterns on skin when used the right way. Or the wrong way. However you want to think of it."

"You're a sadist," he said, his head leaning back against the cross. He looked up as if to seek help from the heavens. Help, unsurprisingly, did not come.

"Flattery will get you everywhere."

She plugged in the wand and held the contact in one hand and the Wartenberg pinwheel in the other. The electricity didn't affect her as she'd made herself merely a conduit. Sparks buzzed from the sharp tips of the wheel, and with a slow and steady pace, she rolled it in a straight line down the center of his chest. He inhaled sharply as the electrified wheel left a thin raised line on his skin. She'd been on the receiving end of this technique before. The wheel never broke the skin, but the combination of electricity and sharp edges made the recipient feel like he was being sliced open.

"Only five lines, I think," she said. "Count them for me. That was..."

"One..." he panted.

She ran the wheel down his chest a second time, then a third. She ran it over the old scars, over his nipples, across the sensitive skin of his lower stomach. When she touched his hipbone with it, he coughed from the pain. He had to say five twice because of how labored his breathing had become.

"Was that five already? Very good."

He exhaled heavily in noticeable relief.

"But let's do one more set. In French. Say *un*," she ordered and ran the wheel once more down his chest.

The sound that escaped his throat was more animal than human. Exactly what she wanted to hear.

By the time they reached *cinq*, he had ten criss-crossing lines on his chest, thin and red as a brand. The welts would fade fairly quickly. The ones produced by the wheel and the wand wouldn't last more than a day or two. Amazing that something that felt like one's chest being cut open by a knife could cause no lasting harm at all.

"On a scale of one to ten," she asked him as she put the wand away and tossed the wheel into the trash can, "what was that?"

"*Onze,*" he said, his eyes closed tight as his whole body shivered from the last aftershocks of the pain.

"*Onze?* I hurt you all the way to eleven? I'm pretty damn proud of myself right now, I have to say." She brought her lips to his chest and licked one of the lines from tip to tip. Her hot mouth against his seared skin must have felt like salt in an open wound. And yet he'd only grown more aroused from this latest round of agony.

Perhaps it was time to put him out of his misery.

She stood face to face with him and pushed her hips into his again. "Your cock is harder than I've ever seen it. And I've seen it hard a lot."

"You have a gift for pain, Maîtresse."

"What can I say? I'm a giver. I'm in a very giving mood right now. Are you in a taking mood?"

"Yes," he breathed, sounding more desperate than she'd ever heard him.

"So you know what a stickler my hard-ass boss is, right? I'm not allowed to sell sex. Only kink. I can only get women off, not the men...."

"I hate your boss. He has no compassion."

"Tell me about it. How's this...I'll charge you for the pain, and the sex will be on the house. How's that?"

"A perfect compromise. Surely not even your boss could find fault with that."

"What he doesn't know won't hurt him." She brought her lips to his mouth.

"Yes...whatever we do," he said, smiling against her mouth, "let's not hurt him."

With a wink, she kissed him long and slow and deep. The kiss felt more wicked than all the pain she'd given him that hour. She was a dominatrix. Pain was her profession. She never kissed her clients. Then again, this was no ordinary client.

She pulled back and grinned at him—almost. "Now I have to get you into the bedroom. How should I lead you there? Leash again?"

"God no, please."

"Then it's on your hands and knees. Down, boy."

With a whistle and a pat on her leg, she summoned him to follow her as if he was a dog. And like a dog he followed behind her on all fours. Once in the bedroom, she grabbed him by the back of his hair and pulled him off the floor.

"Middle of the bed. On your stomach," she said. "Get comfy. I'll be right back."

She lingered in her dungeon a little longer than necessary. He'd waited this long for release.

Why not make him wait a few minutes more? After getting herself ready, tightening the strap-on harness, and gathering her supplies, she sat down, pulled a file out of a drawer, and gave her nails a nice buffing.

Once her fingernails resembled polished glass, she decided to give the poor man in the other room the attention he'd earned.

She returned to the bedroom and, without a word, took his left wrist in her hand. She buckled a cuff on it and secured him to the bedpost with rope and a snap hook. She gave his right arm and both legs the same treatment until he lay face down on the bed, spread-eagled and completely unable to get away. As she crawled over the rich gold and red brocade sheets, she dropped nibbles and kisses from his wrist to his shoulder and down the center of his back, now marbled a red and purple with blood and bruises. She straddled his thigh and lightly tickled his side with her fingertips.

"If I remember correctly, and I do, you've fucked me up the ass a few dozen times. Not very nice of you, considering your cock is bigger than your ego." She picked up the tube of lube, poured some out on her fingertips, and began applying it to him.

"I don't recall you complaining..." He certainly wasn't complaining at the moment. With her fingers inside him, his breathing had turned hoarse and ragged. He inhaled between each word, winced with pleasure at every movement further into him.

"Why would I complain with your cock in my ass?" She pulled her fingers out of him. "That sounds like Christmas come early to me. Oh, by the way, Merry Christmas."

With the dildo in her hand, she pushed into him with one smooth stroke and stopped, pausing only to make him groan with his need.

She started to move and move slowly, letting him open up to her. The man loved anal sex...giving, receiving, watching, all of the above. But he kept his switch side so private that he rarely allowed himself this pleasure. Other men in their community had a bad habit of looking down on male bottoms and submissives. Hypocrites, all of them. They snuck in her dungeon while the world wasn't looking and sat at her feet and begged her to fuck them like this. She beat the shit out of them and sent them on their way. She never even gave them the chance to earn the pleasure she gave this special client so willingly. Those faux-doms with their dick-swinging machismo didn't deserve to be her bitch.

"I'm only doing this because you earned it," she said, pushing into him again. She caressed his shoulders, his sides, read the welts underneath her fingertips like Braille writing. She leaned forward and lay briefly on his back as she continued to work against him. "No other reason."

"None? You don't enjoy it?"

"Hardly. I hate it," she said as a tremor of pleasure ran through her hips. She closed her eyes and dug her fingers into his sides. "Absolutely hate it..."

He laughed at her lies, and she flicked him on the back to punish him.

"No laughing allowed," she said. "Just moaning, groaning, and maybe gasping."

"Gasping?"

She pushed in hard and deep and he gasped.

"Right," she said, giving his back a little bite. "Gasping."

She did love doing this sort of thing, with him especially (although she had a female sub or two she'd nearly fucked unconscious). Nothing in the world more empowering than penetrating another person and fucking them right to the dark and ragged edges where ecstasy intersected with pain.

"Had enough?" she asked as his breathing grew more and more labored.

"Never," he panted.

"Okay. Fine. I'll keep fucking you. I was going to blow you and let you come in my mouth, but whatever. If you insist."

"Can I change my answer?"

"I think you just did."

She pulled out of him and removed her harness, tossing it on the ground with a flourish. Men should be so lucky to have a cock that indestructible.

An hour of pain-play, dominance, and fucking had made her more than ready to have a cock inside her mouth. She stripped him of the bounds, pushed him onto his back, and with her knees, shoved his thighs wide open so she could sit between them. She took him first in her hand and then into her mouth.

She wasn't in a mood to tease him right now, and he was in no mood to be teased. Not anymore. Not after so much pain and erotic torture. He needed to come and she wanted him to come, hard and soon.

With her tongue, she caressed him from base to tip and back again. With her lips, she massaged him. Then she sucked long and deep on him as his hips rose off the bed, pumping into her mouth. She loved the warm taste of him, the size of him, the way he lost himself so utterly in submitting to her. He grasped at the sheets and arched underneath her.

Nudging his thighs a little wider, she pushed two fingers into him. She kneaded all his favorite spots inside him with just the right amount of pressure to bring his shoulders off the bed and send him coming into her mouth.

She received every drop of what he had to give her and took him in with one swallow.

"Feel better, Slut?" She crawled up his body and straddled his chest, sitting on his stomach.

"Much. *Merci*, Maîtresse."

"For you, anytime." She grabbed his hands and pushed his wrists back into the pillows. "As long as you pay me, of course."

"Of course."

Bending down, she gave him one more kiss, letting him taste himself on her mouth.

"I suppose I need to clean you up." She sat up again and gave him an appraising look. He was beaten, bloody, and covered in lube. Pretty typical evening for both of them.

"I would appreciate it."

"I could give you a bath. A nice long hot bubble bath. Maybe some vanilla-scented soap?"

"You wouldn't dare." He grimaced at her.

"I might. You still have my mask on. You're still my pretty submissive."

"I can't take anymore," he said, and she detected a rare note of sincerity in his voice. "Have you no mercy?"

"No. Not usually. But for you...maybe a little." She winked at him and gave him one more kiss. "No bubble bath. I'll get the basin and some warm water. I'll clean the blood off. I think we're going to need the first aid kit."

"If we ever have a session where we don't need the first aid kit, I'll find a new dominatrix."

"I can't have that. You're my worst tipper and still my favorite client. Don't tell The Boss though. He says I can't play favorites."

"Your secret is safe with me."

"And yours are safe with me. Always," The Mistress said, tracing his full bottom lip with her thumb. She would guard his secrets with her life. It took so much courage for a man to admit to his submissive side. The last thing she wanted to do was betray him after he'd made himself so vulnerable to her. He kept her secrets as she kept his. He knew she still bottomed every now and then. At the clubs and in the scene, they billed her as a "former submissive" or "ex-submissive." Sometimes, a "reformed submissive." But there was no "ex" or "former" for her. And God knew she'd walk into Hell before she let anyone "re-form" her. No, just like him, The Mistress was a switch.

"*Merci.*" He kissed her palm and she smiled down at him.

"Bad boy. I'm going to add an extra hundred onto your bill for that kiss. You know The Boss's rule: I touch the clients, the clients do not touch me."

"All apologies. I'll never do it again."

"See that you don't." She flicked the tip of his nose and scooted off the bed.

* * *

In the other room, she found her large metal basin and filled it with warm water. She grabbed soap and her softest towel before returning to the bedroom. When she went to set the basin on the side table, she made the mistake of turning her back to him for all of five seconds. In that five seconds, she saw something fall to the floor at her feet.

The black mask.

"Don't..." she warned, but the warning went unheeded. Before she could turn back around, two strong arms encircled her and dragged her down to the bed.

"No mask. Not your sub anymore." He pushed her down deep into the sheets, holding her by her wrists and the force of his body weight.

"Stop it," she ordered, struggling underneath him. Her struggles were in vain. He might have a submissive and masochistic side to him, but there was no part of him anyone could call weak. Not anyone without a deathwish anyway.

"Make me." He forced her legs apart with his knees. With one hand he ripped at her corset, baring her breasts and savaging them with hungry kisses. The harder she fought back against him, the more viselike his grip on her became. He sucked on her nipples, kissed and bit her neck. Abruptly, he released her. Before she could get away from him, he grabbed her again, reached under her skirt, and yanked her black lace panties. They came off after two hard tears and wound up with the mask on the floor. Fucking him had made her so wet it barely hurt when he shoved his fingers into her. His cold, arrogant laugh stung more than the intrusion into her body. "I think you've enjoyed this little session as much as I have."

"I *was* enjoying it," she said through gritted teeth as he pushed a fourth finger into her. He stretched her with his hand and fucked her with his fingers. Her pride demanded she hate the penetration, but her body and her pride and her vagina were rarely on speaking terms. She grasped at the headboard, trying to find a means of escaping him. His thumb violated her anally while his fingers probed deep inside her vagina. If the bastard made her orgasm, she would never forgive herself. "Not enjoying it anymore."

"Liar."

He pulled his hand out of her, flipped her onto her stomach, and held her down by her shoulders. When he entered her, she put up one more fight. A useless attempt because nothing could stop his thrusts now that he was inside her. Settling down, she gave up and let him have her. How could she fight anymore when every movement sent fissures of unholy pleasure shooting through her back, stomach, and thighs. Underneath him, she panted and moaned, writhed like a whore showing off for her best customer. She heard his labored breathing at the back of her neck, felt his teeth against her skin. And inside her she felt him filling her completely, so completely she could only spread her legs even wider to take him all in.

"You know you love submitting even more than I do," he taunted. "Admit it."

"No."

"Then why are you so wet I can hear it?"

"It's a water bed," she said, and he laughed into her ear.

Even laughing, he didn't let up. He fucked her like she'd beaten him—brutally and without mercy and for what felt like eternity. He'd already come once, so this time she was in for it. From personal experience she knew his second orgasm would be a long time coming. Part of her wanted to simply let go and let him win. But every few minutes she'd remember that this was happening in her dungeon, where she was supposed to be in charge. Waiting until she could be sure he was lost in the haze of sex, she tried to raise up and force him off of her. But he clamped a hand down on the back of her neck, shoved her back down onto the bed, and rode her even harder.

With his fingers digging into her neck with

bruising force, that secret submissive part of her rose up and took control of every part of her from the waist down. Entirely against her will she came, loud and lusty. A few minutes later, he reached around her hip, found her clitoris and stroked her to a second and even more humiliating climax.

At last, she felt his thrusts slowing and growing harder. He pulled out but only long enough to put her flat on her back and push into her again.

"Oh don't you fucking dare," she said, trying and failing to squirm away from him. But she couldn't get away and she could do nothing but lay on her back, held down by his incredible strength as he pushed and pushed and pushed into her. He closed his eyes and pulled out of her. He ripped the condom off and threw it aside. When he came, it was on her, the warm fluid spurting onto her breasts.

With a sigh, he collapsed on top of her. She wrapped her arms and legs around him and rolled him onto his back.

"You realize I'm going to kill you the next time you submit to me. You know that right?" She grabbed the towel off the nightstand, soaked it in the water that had gone cold, and wiped his semen off her. "No more breath-play. It's death-play next time. You come to my dungeon. I kill you."

"It was worth it," he grinned devilishly at her and she fought the urge to slap that shit-eating grin off his face.

"You know this is the reason why people don't trust switches. That little stunt you pulled just now?"

"Fucking you raw when you least expected it, you mean?"

"That one. That's why normal kinky people don't like us." She tossed the towel into the basin and straightened her corset.

"I like us," he said, turning over again, and resting on his elbows. "You don't?"

"No, I don't like us." She grabbed him by the back of the neck and gave him a bruising kiss and a skin-breaking bite to his bottom lip. "I fucking love us...Boss."

* * *

So there ya go, King. You wanted a recitation of one of our sessions together, and here it is. You are easily the most narcissistic man on the planet. Could you please make sure this file goes into the Confidential Coded cabinets? Or at least into your private porn collection? I'd really not like it if it got out that I've fucked a client. Or, more accurately, let one fuck me. I should have safed out right before you came on me just to piss you off. And I would have, except you're annoyingly good at rough fucking. Seriously. Do they teach you guys that in French high schools? If so, I'm booking a trip to Paris tomorrow.

In conclusion, you are the single most frustrating, dangerous, exhausting, overbearing, irritating client on my entire roster (and that includes the medical fetishist who makes me dress like Florence Nightingale and speak in an English accent).

That being said...I'm free tomorrow night.

FILE #5

Client Name: Chris McKay i.e. "The New Sam" (age 23)

Profession: Head bartender at the Möbius Strip Club

Inclination: Vanilla

Level of Experience: None

Orientation: Lesbian (the sexy-cute androgynous kind that looks like a teenaged boy—I'm sure there's an actual term for that but I left my LGBTQ dictionary at home)

* * *

When you have a sexual problem in New York City, and you don't know who to ask for help, you go to Kingsley Edge. He might not know the answer, but he knows someone who does. In this case, he knew me.

I'll admit, this client was a weird one. Not her, she wasn't weird. The job was weird. Never done this sort of thing before, and I'm fairly certain I'll never do it again. Not because I don't want to—I rather enjoyed it—but because my client was something of a one-of-a-kind despite her unofficial job title.

Very few of my clients are women. Perhaps only 1% of those who come to me alone. I see a few more with couples, but single women can usually get the kink they need at play parties without having to pay for it. This particular woman, however, was a special case. I only saw her in my dungeon once.

I'll never see her in my dungeon again.

After all, this client wasn't kinky. And yet, she still needed me.

The Mistress headed to her dungeon and found her client waiting outside the door. The client wasn't alone, however. She had a man with her— a handsome man wearing a gray suit vaguely Regency-era and black riding boots. The client and the man spoke in hushed tones back and forth to each other. It seemed the man was trying to comfort the woman or give her some words of encouragement. As The Mistress strode down the hall toward them, she studied her new client, Chris. The young woman wore skinny jeans, a white t-shirt, a black leather jacket, battered Docs, and her sexy short black hair had been artfully coiffed. From a distance, she looked a lot like a teenage boy circa 1956. Up close, she looked like a stunningly beautiful woman who did everything she could in her power to look like a teenage boy circa 1956.

"So this is the New Sam?" The Mistress asked as she unlocked her dungeon door.

"She is indeed," Kingsley, the man in the riding boots said with pride.

Chris rolled her eyes. Apparently this was a conversation she'd heard once too often.

"I'm Chris."

The Mistress shook her hand. "Very nice to beat you."

"Beat me? I didn't think..."

"She's joking." Kingsley put his arm around Chris's shoulder like a protective older brother and ushered her into the first room of the dungeon. "It's her line. It's an old line, and she should get some new lines."

"You start paying me more and maybe I can afford some new lines, King. Now shoo. We've got girl stuff to do." She tried waving him out of her dungeon, but he didn't budge.

"I'm not leaving until Chris tells me she wants me gone. I'll stay the entire time if she needs me." He gave The Mistress a pointed look, one The Mistress returned even more pointedly. If they didn't stop staring pointedly at each other, one of them was going to lose an eye.

"I'm fine. Seriously," Chris said, although she didn't sound one-hundred percent sure.

"I can stay out here if you want. You can have your privacy and know I'm only a room away." He looked into her eyes as if trying to read them.

Chris smiled. "Seriously, I'm good. I can do this."

The Mistress snapped her fingers in his face. "Stop acting all fatherly. She's in good hands. I'll get her back to you in one piece. Now this is personal shit she and I need to do. No men allowed. Skedaddle."

"Did you just tell me to 'skedaddle'?" Kingsley said, his French accent struggling with the word.

"I did. And I mean it. Chris?"

"She means it. We win. You lose. Shoo."

"*C'est la guerre.* I'm going." Kingsley didn't sound like he wanted to leave, but the man was smart enough to know when he was outnumbered. "I'll be back in an hour to take Chris home. Is that long enough?"

"If it isn't, then you can wait in the hallway until she comes out. *Oui?*" The Mistress gave him an entirely insincere smile.

"You don't have to escort me home. I'll be okay." Chris rolled her eyes again. The Mistress had a feeling this scenario played out fairly often. Kingsley did get a bit overprotective of his Sams. She had to wonder if the Original Sam knew what she'd done to the man.

"I know you'll be fine. I'm taking you home anyway."

"Fine. Fine." Chris raised her hands in surrender.

"Yes, it's all fine. Now go, Dad. Time for the slumber party. Out."

Kingsley raised Chris's hand and kissed the back of it before giving The Mistress one last menacing look. "Take good care of her," he ordered. *"Non.* Take the best care of her."

"She gets my A-game. You get out."

With one more bow, Kingsley left the room.

"God damn, that man is such a mother hen sometimes." The Mistress opened the door to make sure he'd really gone. She wouldn't put it past him to wait out in the hallway the entire time.

"He is, and I have no idea why," Chris said. "He's so weird."

The Mistress waved her hand dismissively. "He's French."

"It's not that. He treats me like a princess. Do I look like a princess to you?" Chris motioned at herself to indicate her short spiky hair, her boyish clothes and boots.

"You're the New Sam. You might as well be royalty to him."

"That might explain things if I knew what the hell that meant." Chris looked around and nodded her approval. The Mistress did have a rather swank set-up in the front room of her suite. But what they needed for their session was in the second room, the play-room.

"You don't know about Sam?" The Mistress

led Chris to the examination bed she had for her medical fetishists. She patted the seat to indicate Chris should sit, and then The Mistress took a seat on a wheeled stool across from her.

"No. Everyone says, 'Oh, you must be the New Sam' when they meet me, but no one's told me who she or he or what a Sam is."

"Take your shoes, pants, and underwear off, get under the sheet, and then I'll tell you."

Chris seemed just nervous enough that The Mistress decided she might need to try a little carrot-stick action to get her client to relax and undress. Stick: taking her clothes off in front of a stranger. Carrot: the answer to her long-held question.

"Um...okay. You gonna watch?" Chris asked, clearly embarrassed.

"I am. I'm a dominatrix, not a doctor. Unless you absolutely need me to leave the room, I'm staying in here. I'm going to see what's under the clothes anyway, so I don't know how not letting me watch you undress is going to save you any modesty points. And the sooner you get used to being naked around me, the better. You aren't submitting to me, however, so you can ask me to leave if you need me to."

Chris exhaled heavily and dangled her feet over the edge of the bed like a nervous child. "Fine. Whatever. You're right. You're gonna see everything anyway," she said, raising her legs to start unlacing her boots.

"Good girl."

"Good girl?"

"Sorry. Habit. I'll turn the heat up in here so you can relax more."

The Mistress clicked the temperature up a few notches while Chris shimmied out her jeans and underwear. For a young woman trying very hard to go the butch route, she had on remarkably pretty panties, white and lace-trimmed. Boyshorts-style, but still quite girly. And although she couldn't have weighed more than a hundred-and-ten pounds, she had some good curves on her. Nice hips, shapely legs. Her pubic hair had been close-trimmed but not shaved or waxed off. Nice to see a woman who wasn't afraid of looking like an actual adult under her clothes.

"Okay, just lay back. We'll take our time here," The Mistress said as she sanitized her hands thoroughly. She raised the stirrups on the examining table and helped Chris get her feet into them. "I won't touch you without warning you first. Cool?"

"Cool." Chris took a slow breath and stared up at the ceiling.

"Cool. I'll get the toys. Don't be freaked out." The Mistress pulled open a drawer and one by one removed six dildos of varying sizes and lined

THE CASE OF THE BROKENHEARTED BARTENDER / 153

them up on the metal tray. Chris watched her the entire time, her eyes growing wider as dildos of impressive size appeared.

"Holy shit," Chris breathed as she took in the array. "That big?"

"Never seen one before? I mean, an actual penis on a grown man?"

"Not in person. Only pictures. I'm a gold-star lesbian," she said with pride.

"Gold star?" The Mistress pulled out some gauze pads and a small bullet vibrator.

"That's what you call someone gay or lesbian who's never been with the opposite sex. I knew what I was in kindergarten. Never had any confusion about what I was, so never fooled around with a guy at all."

"Nice. I'm a gold-star kinkster then. Never had vanilla sex."

"Wow. I think that would be a lot harder than a gold-star lesbian. Kinky sex looks like a lot of work." She glanced around the dungeon, at the various ropes, floggers, single-tails, and other implements of torture hanging on the walls.

The Mistress sat back down on the stool and scooted in closer to Chris. "It's probably more work than vanilla sex, but completely worth it. You take sex more seriously when you have to plan it in advance, do equipment checks, and have a medic on standby. It's the price we pay if we want our gold stars."

"I guess I'm paying the price for being a gold star. This is probably the most embarrassing thing ever."

"Don't be embarrassed. Not allowed around me. Unless it's one of your kinks."

"I'm twenty-three, and I'm not a virgin," Chris said. "I've been having sex with girls since I was sixteen."

"You don't have to feel bad. An intact hymen isn't a badge of shame."

"It's a pain in the ass is what it is."

The Mistress looked at Chris over the sheet. "If your hymen is a pain in the ass, then we're going to rethink our hymen-breaking strategy here. That's okay. I have butt-plugs galore."

Chris covered her face with one hand and laughed ruefully. "Sorry," she said, leaning up on her elbows. "Pain in the vadge? Is that better?"

"I don't know if it's better, but it certainly makes more sense anatomically. You want to get started?"

"Not really." Chris lay flat on her back again. "But I'd rather get it over with as soon as possible."

The Mistress pulled her stool up even closer and adjusted the sheet and her light. "I'm going to touch you now. Just one finger inside. Want to see what you've got under the hood so to speak."

"Go for it," Chris said with a heavy sigh.

"You know, usually when I fingerbang girls,

they sound a lot more happy about it." The Mistress spread Chris's folds open and slipped one finger into her. "Does that hurt?"

Chris shook her head. "That's fine. I use tampons so I'm used to something finger-sized."

"But not much more than that. Jesus, you are tight. I thought I had the hymen from hell. No wonder you've been putting this off."

"I've tried breaking it a few times myself, and I just can't. Hurts too much."

The Mistress pressed down against the layers of tissue at the opening of Chris's vagina. Breaking that killer hymen would take more than just a couple minutes with a vibrator.

"I don't blame you. In my world there's good pain and bad pain. Getting your vagina ripped is of the 'bad pain' variety. Are you sure you want to do this? Sober, I mean? I can get some booze or drugs. God only knows what's in King's medicine cabinet right now."

"King gave me a Vicodin to take after if I needed it. I better not take anything else."

"You sure about doing this?"

"I'm sure. I need to do it."

The Mistress heard a note of sadness in the girl's voice. "Need to?"

Chris nodded. "Need. My girlfriend—ex-girlfriend now—accused me of being 'stone-cold.'"

The Mistress looked up over the sheet at Chris. "You're going to have to explain that one to me. I can barely keep up with all the different permutations of kinky people. I'll need the Cliffs-Notes on the lesbians." The Mistress moved her finger gently in and out of Chris simply to get her accustomed to being touched so intimately.

"Stone-cold? It's, um..." Chris paused to think. "There are some of us who are really masculine. So a stone-cold lesbian, she doesn't want her body treated like, you know, a man would treat a woman."

"So no penetration?"

"Right. Exactly. It's not a bad thing, usually."

"So your ex-girlfriend called you stone-cold because you don't like being penetrated?"

"It was more than that. I never even let her try. Being twenty-three and sexually active and having the hymen of a ten-year-old girl is humiliating. I didn't want to deal with her having to deal with me. More than one finger hurts, so what's the point? Anyway, Theresa said she couldn't be with someone so closed-off. We started fighting a lot. I thought everything was great between us...except in bed. Apparently sex mattered more than everything else to her."

"Sex does matter in a relationship. If Theresa had needs you couldn't meet—"

"I know, I know. But I didn't think it was the be-all, end-all of our relationship."

"Do you want to be penetrated, or are you happy being—"

"I want it. I do. I just…can't."

The Mistress pulled her hand out and held up two fingers. Chris nodded her agreement, and The Mistress pushed into her again gently. Chris winced only once.

"Sex in a relationship is a partnership," The Mistress said. "One person can't do all the work. And you're being fingered by a woman who used to submit to the most dominant of all dominant men. He's not an alpha male—he's the alpha and omega male. He met the president once and the president called him 'Sir.' Even in that relationship with Captain Über-Dom, we both did the work in the bedroom. Or the kitchen. Or the living room. Or the dungeon. Or under the piano…"

"Under?"

"He wouldn't do me on top of the piano. He didn't want me scratching the finish."

"Makes sense."

"The point is, I told him things I enjoyed, and we did them. He told me things he wanted to try and we did them. I loved his body, so he let me touch him any way I wanted. He loved mine. No part of me was off-limits to him. I'm sure Theresa wanted to give you the sort of pleasure you gave her. One partner doing all the work while the other one lays there is nice…for a night or two. After that, it gets old. And you start to feel like, 'What's wrong with me? Why doesn't he/she/they want me to touch her?' Any chance Theresa felt like you didn't want her touching you?"

"Um...maybe?"

"More than maybe?"

"I did sort of say something to the effect of, 'I don't want you in me.'"

"I'm in you. Is it really that awful?" The Mistress raised her eyebrow at Chris.

"No. Not awful. A little weird. Not used to it. But it's not bad."

"Not bad? All I get is a 'not bad'? I better kick this orgy up a notch or two." She stood up between Chris's legs and reached for the smallest of her vibrators, the one that fit over the end of her finger.

"What is that?" Chris eyed The Mistress's hand warily.

"Tiny vibrator. Don't worry. It's not going in you. A little clitoral stimulation helps the dildo go down. Try to relax. You'll enjoy this."

Chris laid back on the table again and gazed up at the ceiling. "I hadn't planned on enjoying this experience."

"If you didn't want pleasure with your pain, you should have gone to a doctor, not a dominatrix." The Mistress turned the vibrator on and started to massage near Chris's clitoris.

"I went to a doctor. Want to know what she told me?"

The Mistress winced. "From the tone of your voice I'm guessing I don't. But tell me anyway."

"She told me to break my hymen the old-fashioned way, by having sex with a man. She said I only needed to do it once. Close my eyes and think of England, she said."

"What a homophobic bitch. I hope you reported her to the medical board."

"Kingsley did when I told him. He's determined to get her censured or whatever they do."

"Good for King. I'm not at all surprised you decided to go a different route after that run-in. Yeah, doctors don't know what to do with people like us sometimes. I used to sub a lot and would get minor injuries every now and then. Kingsley always sent me to a kinky doctor so I wouldn't have to deal with the inevitable phone calls to the police and psych evaluations."

"Kingsley's cool. You know, for a man. I almost...well, not almost. But it crossed my mind." Chris blushed bright red and The Mistress bit back a smile.

"It's a good thing you didn't. He'd probably say no. He's not in the habit of having sex with anyone who isn't one-hundred percent into it. And even if he did agree...."

The Mistress paused and picked up the second largest of the dildos on her tray. She held it up for Chris to see.

"Oh my God. Are you serious?" Chris looked like she'd pass out from the sight of it.

"Serious." She put the dildo back on the tray. "The man's cock is as big as his ego."

"That's huge."

"Tell me about it."

"I can't believe straight women can take something like that."

The Mistress laughed. "Don't get all prudish on me. You aren't my first lady who loves the ladies I've had in here. Some of the sisterhood can take an arm up to the elbow. I know this from personal experience."

"You're bi?" Chris sounded dubious.

"Let's just say the Hard Rock Cafe and I have one thing in common. We love all and serve all."

"Nice."

"But to answer your question, yes. I sleep with men and women. Was in a fairly long-term relationship with a woman a few years ago. We broke up."

"What happened?"

"She decided to stay a nun. I have got to stop dating people in religious orders."

Chris laughed again, and The Mistress let her laugh even though she hadn't been joking. Instead, she silenced Chris's laughter by pressing the fingertip vibrator to her clitoris.

Chris gasped a little and balled her fingers tight into a fist. "Oh, wow."

"Fun, right?"

"Kind of fun. Definitely."

"Good. When you start to feel pain, just focus your attention on your clitoris and all the fun in that area, okay?"

Chris nodded and closed her eyes.

"So..." The Mistress asked as she pushed down on the back of Chris's vagina again, pressing against the hymen. "Are you doing this for your ex-girlfriend or for you?"

"I'm doing this for me. I've wanted to do it a long time. I had a girlfriend before Theresa, but she didn't complain about me not wanting any penetration. But she was kind of selfish. Very selfish in bed and out. It wasn't until Theresa that I started to think about it. She was okay with our sex life at first, but it really hurt her that I wouldn't let her inside me. Hurt her enough that she dumped me. The break-up was the final straw. That and Kingsley catching me sobbing in my rum and Coke after closing bell three nights ago."

"Kingsley cannot resist a woman in distress. Especially his New Sam."

"Okay, you have to tell me who the fuck this Sam person is and why everyone talks about her like she's some kind of dearly-departed saint."

The Mistress laughed so hard it seemed to startle Chris. Somewhere Sam's ears were burning at the combination of her name and "saint" in the same sentence.

"Sam was the first head bartender at the Möbius. The old owner had the brilliant idea that he needed lesbian bartenders. Straight male bartenders would hit on the strippers. Gay male bartenders would hit on the customers. Girlie women bartenders would get hit on by the customers..."

"So a butchy looking lesbian was his bright idea?"

"Exactly," The Mistress said as she slowly pulled her two fingers out of Chris.

"That's actually pretty brilliant."

"It was. Sam kept everybody in line."

"I do the same thing. At least I try to. Just because they're strippers doesn't mean anyone gets to disrespect them. I have a zero-tolerance policy for bad behavior."

"Good girl. Sam instituted the same policy. Nobody crossed Sam. Not even Kingsley after he bought the place and changed the name."

"I like this Sam person."

"You would like her. Wish she still lived here. Sam looked a little like you—skinny twerp, very pretty in a 'I want to be mistaken for a fourteen-year-old boy' way."

"That's so not true. I look nothing like a fourteen-year-old boy. Just so happens a lot of fourteen-year-old boys look like me."

"At least Sam didn't dress like any fourteen-year-old boy I'd seen. I was just a teenager when Sam ran the Möbius. But every time I saw her she had on a suit—an old-fashioned one, with a vest and suspenders. No jackets though. It killed me when I saw her. Wanted to snap those sexy suspenders of hers."

"Damn. I gotta hunt up a pic of her."

"She even wore spats on her dress shoes. Actual spats. She said it wasn't a fashion statement, but a necessity for anyone who worked at a strip club." The Mistress moved the vibrator over Chris's clitoris as she started to push the smallest of the dildos into her.

"Smart woman."

"She was. Still is. I mean, she's not dead."

"That's comforting. The way people talk about her..."

"I know. She kind of still haunts the place. Sam started as a bartender at the Möbius when she was about your age. After buying the Möbius, Kingsley started putting together a new club. An underground S&M club. *The* underground S&M club to end all S&M clubs. This S&M club that we're in, as a matter of fact. And it took a lot of work. He decided he needed an assistant. He'd lost his five previous assistants in as many months."

"Why? Kingsley's the best boss I've ever had. Pays double what I'd make bartending anywhere else. Good benefits. And he's nice to me—weirdly nice to me—and stays out of my way. He trusts my decisions. Plus, he's the one who sent me to you and is picking up the tab for this session."

The Mistress pushed the small dildo all the way into Chris. She winced again and breathed but seemed to be taking it in stride.

"Well, you have to understand the situation here. You are a gold star lesbian. Kingsley's a gold star seducer. Male assistant, female assistant. Didn't matter. He slept with them all. Lots of drama with him in his household in the early days. Love, lust, fighting, jealously. He'd sleep with his secretary, and then the next day she'd find him making out with some hot guy in the hallway. Big blow-up. She'd quit. He'd start assistant-hunting again. The cycle would start over."

"So a lesbian was his only option?" Chris seemed amused by the idea.

"Well, he knew she was the one woman on his payroll who wouldn't try to seduce him and he wouldn't try to seduce. He stole her from the Möbius and made her his second-in-command. Match made in heaven. Those two were inseparable—best friends, although sometimes it was hard to tell that. Sam wasn't just a bartender, she was a genius. Kingsley didn't scare her, so she stood up to him. She worked her ass off and earned the respect of everyone in The Underground. If Sam spoke, you did what she said as if Kingsley himself had given the order."

"No wonder everyone does what I tell them to. They think it's coming from Kingsley."

"If you work for Kingsley and he respects you, he'll back you up all the way to the edge of the world. Even if you're wrong, he'll still take your side. He's really loyal to his employees. And now that he's stopped fucking them left and right, they're loyal back."

"So me being 'The New Sam' is a good thing?"

"It's a very good thing. Kingsley...he loved Sam. Wasn't in love with her, but she was probably the first and only woman he'd never slept with that he truly loved. They were a perfect team."

"What happened to her? To them?"

"Only good things, I promise. But even good things sometimes mean sacrifices, giving up the good for the better. Kingsley has Juliette as his second-in-command now, so he leaves the New Sams in charge at the Möbius. Juliette's even scarier than a lesbian." The Mistress gave Chris a smile so she would know she was joking. But Chris seemed entirely lost in what was happening under the sheet. "You're enjoying this, aren't you?"

Chris smiled. "A little. It hurt some at first but it's...yeah, that's pretty enjoyable."

"Enjoyable? Okay, well, that's a start. I'm trying to remember if a guy ever told me 'that's enjoyable' during a blow-job. Give me a minute because that's a considerable mental Rolodex I'm flipping through."

When Chris laughed, the dildo nearly came out of her.

"Shit," The Mistress said, pushing it back in. "Nice PC muscles."

"You know, that might be the first time anyone's complimented my PC muscles before."

"The stronger the PC muscles, the stronger the orgasms. I do Kegels all the time."

"Do they work?" Chris asked.

"I could crack a walnut."

Chris burst into laughter again, and The Mistress took advantage of that momentary distraction to push a larger dildo into her. The laughter stopped as Chris closed her eyes tight.

"I know it hurts. Just try to focus on the pleasure, okay?" The Mistress turned the fingertip vibrator onto a higher setting.

"Now you know why I've been putting this off."

"I don't blame you. Since you don't have sex with men, there's no real reason to even worry about your hymen. Unless you plan on using toys or doing fisting or..."

"I never planned on any of that. No toys. No dildos. Too much baggage."

The Mistress moved the dildo slowly in and out of Chris and rotated it in circles, trying to widen the tight hole. "Baggage? What kind of toys are you using?"

"You know what I mean. A lot of us don't like using stuff like that, stuff that's just a penis replacement. We don't need that. And we don't need anyone thinking gay women have penis envy."

"I don't think what you and your girlfriend do in the privacy of your bedroom has anything to do with what a bunch of ignorant homophobes say about you. These are the same people who think God invented AIDS to punish gay people, conveniently forgetting that lesbians have the lowest rate of STD infection in the entire world."

"It's not just them. Sometimes, other queer women get judgmental about it too. Like you're less of a lesbian if you use toys and stuff."

"It's your body and your bed. You make the rules. Straight couples use toys and vibrators all the time to amp things up even though there's already a cock present and accounted for. You've got to stop thinking of toys as stand-ins for penises. The penis is shaped like this, right?" The Mistress held up two fingers. "Penises are stand-ins for fingers."

"That's one way to think of it."

"Most women I know can't come from straight penis-in-vagina sex anyway. They need clitoral and g-spot stimulation and a lot of foreplay in general. So the superiority of PIV sex is greatly exaggerated."

"That's good to hear."

"I love PIV, but even I need more than just penetration and thrusting usually."

"Like what?"

"Flogging. Bondage. But even I know that's not typical foreplay. A typical woman I am not."

"I can see that. I've never seen a dominatrix in a Pearl Jam t-shirt before."

"Considering you aren't kinky, I didn't think you needed me in eight-inch stiletto boots and a leather bustier to pop your cherry."

"The jeans and t-shirt is a great look for you. You're gorgeous. Your eyes keep changing colors. That's crazy."

The Mistress arched an eyebrow at her. "Behave there. Just because you're spread out on my table and I'm fucking you with a vibrator and a dildo doesn't mean you can hit on me."

"It doesn't?"

"Okay, it does. Tell me more about my eyes." The Mistress batted her eyelashes at Chris in the hopes of getting her to laugh again. Anything to distract her from the next step up in dildo size.

But Chris didn't laugh. She stared at The Mistress instead, studied her, and not in a detached sort of way. The Mistress knew heat when she saw it. Good. The more turned-on Chris was during this whole process, the better.

"They're beautiful," Chris said without even breaking a smile. "All of you is. But you probably hear that a lot."

"I do but usually just from my male submissive clients. And then only when I order them to tell me how much they worship me. Great job. Good for the self-esteem." The Mistress picked up the next largest-sized dildo and slowly and carefully inserted it into Chris. Chris raised her hips as it went it, a good sign.

"I can't really see you having any self-esteem issues."

"I'm pretty fond of me. You might be a little fonder of yourself if you were more comfortable with your body."

"I am totally comfortable with my body. I like the way I look."

"You should. You're sexy as hell. But you're also twenty-three years old, you've been sexually active for seven years now, and this is the first time you've let a woman inside you. Being comfortable with your body isn't just about the way you look. You have to be willing to admit that people are attracted to you, that a woman who loves you is going to want to touch you and be inside you.

"You can't be the only one giving the pleasure and then shut yourself off to receiving it. That's not fair to your partner. I hang around with a lot of male subs. These are men who genuinely love giving orgasms and oral sex more than they do receiving it. Burying their face in a pussy is their version of heaven. You tell them they can't go down on you, can't pleasure you, and they'll drop you for a new domme so fast your ass will bruise from the fall. They don't want to be with a woman who doesn't let them do the job they feel they were born for—pleasuring women.

"Theresa probably felt the same way about you. She might love fisting and hand jobs and playing with toys and giving the woman she loves orgasms. Did you ever think about that?"

Chris sighed and rested back on the bed again. "No...not really. I thought she'd appreciate me doing all the work."

"Chris, baby, gorgeous...look at me."

Chris raised her head as The Mistress pressed the dildo down into the most stubborn part of her hymen.

"I'm a motherfucking dominatrix, sweetheart, and not even I want to be in charge all the time. Got me?"

"Got you."

"Good. Now tell me how we're doing here? Pain?"

Chris exhaled through her nose. "Yes, but not

a ton. It kind of burns. I thought it would feel more like tearing."

"You are tearing."

"I am?"

The Mistress picked up one of the gauze pads and pressed it to Chris's vulva. She held it up. "See? Blood. Not much though."

"I'm bleeding?"

"A little," The Mistress said, throwing it in the trash.

"That doesn't freak you out?"

"Takes more than a little blood to freak out a professional sadist. Quite frankly, it takes more than a lot of blood. Plus everything is sanitized. Everything in this dungeon is clean. The only thing you'll catch from me is a little flak for being so uptight about getting penetrated. And that's nothing but tough love."

"I appreciate the tough love. Usually I'm the one dishing it out."

"Today is the day you learn to take it. Ready to take it?"

"Yes. I think."

The Mistress pursed her lips at Chris.

"Okay, yes. Definitely."

"Good girl." The Mistress picked up the Kingsley-sized dildo and turned the fingertip vibrator up to its highest setting. "Now take a deep breath and on the count of three, blow out hard."

Chris nodded. "One...two...three..."

She pushed out air and The Mistress pushed in. For the first time, Chris let out a genuine cry of pain.

"I know it hurts. I'm sorry," The Mistress said with genuine sympathy. "It sucks being a woman sometimes."

"It really does." Chris spoke through gritted teeth. "God damn..."

"Breathe, just breathe for me. My first time hurt like hell too."

"I think there is a major design flaw in the vagina."

"I won't argue with that," The Mistress said, laughing. She held the dildo inside Chris with her left-hand thumb while she grabbed more gauze with her right hand. The blood was still minimal, but that last thrust had definitely done the trick. "We have fucking periods, cramps, hymens, and that's the pain not even associated with childbirth. We won't even get into that bullshit."

Chris laughed a little even as tears rimmed her eyes. "So unfair."

"But..." The Mistress began as she slowly pulled the large dildo out of Chris and sat it aside.

"But what?"

"There are some perks to being a woman."

"Like what?" Chris sounded skeptical. The

Mistress took out a tube of K-Y lubricant and squeezed it out on her fingers.

"Well…Unlike most men, women can have an almost endless series of orgasms. Men run out of steam a lot faster than we do. They're like old Lincoln Town Cars. Total gas guzzlers. Their tanks go empty real damn fast. Women are like electric battery cars. We can go forever once we're charged up."

"Sounds nice. I should get something battery-operated, maybe."

"Oh honey, I've got more vibrators in this dungeon than Babes In Toyland has in their stockroom. I'll give you one. Never before used, I promise. We'll add it to Kingsley's bill. It'll save you the embarrassment of having to go buy one."

"Thank you. But Kingsley's picking me up, remember?"

"Fine. I'll have one of the male subs around here deliver it to your place later tonight. I'll pay him with a flogging."

"Thank you. I appreciate that. Getting drunk and confessing my hymen issues to Kingsley needs to be the most embarrassing thing I've done this week. I think walking around carrying a vibrator would be the only thing worse."

"You don't know Kingsley very well. He'd probably give you more pointers about the vibe than I could," The Mistress said as she pushed her lube-covered fingers into Chris. The cool liquid was meant to help soothe the soreness. "I'll send you an insertable kind. Sometimes the hymen heals closed. You'll want to keep that from happening."

"You mean it's medically-expedient for me to use a vibrator?"

"Doctor's orders," The Mistress said, massaging inside Chris. With the vibrator on her clitoris and only two fingers inside her vagina, Chris started to pant a little. "And use it to orgasm too. Don't think of it as a substitute penis. Lesbians who use vibrators do not have penis envy. Penises have vibrator envy. Okay?"

"Okay."

"More doctor's orders—lay there and close your eyes. After all you've been through today, you deserve an orgasm."

"You're going to give me an orgasm?"

"Why not? Any objections?"

"No...I guess not."

"You have a freshly opened vagina. We need to take it for a test drive."

"You're really into cars, aren't you?"

"Oh honey, you have no idea..." The Mistress rubbed the tips of her fingers into Chris's g-spot. Chris's head fell back and her hands clenched at the sheet again, this time in obvious pleasure and not pain. The Mistress took her time, exploring inside Chris, touching everything inside her with gently probing fingers. She poured out more lube and inserted three fingers back into her. The pain didn't even seem to register on Chris. A soft moan escaped her lips, a shudder passed through her body.

"Good?"

"Very good," Chris said, a slightly breathy purr in her voice.

"You have to admit there's something to be said for laying there and letting someone pleasure you."

"I'm starting to see, I mean, feel that."

The Mistress focused all her attention on giving Chris as much pleasure as possible. She teased her clitoris, spread her fingers inside her, thrust in and out carefully with her hand. She took her fingers out and pushed in a smaller insertable-style vibrator. Chris's back arched off the table. The Mistress loved her female clients. With her male clients, she never gave handjobs, never had sex with them. She poured pain onto them and into them and if they wanted to come, they handled that themselves while she watched and gave orders.

Giving orgasms to female clients, however, felt like a public service. A pubic service, even.

For the next five minutes, The Mistress focused all her concentration on Chris's pleasure, bringing her close to orgasm and pulling back again, pushing her to the edge and then pulling back. The Mistress wanted to make Chris come so hard her IQ dropped and her face melted.

"Don't come yet..." The Mistress said. "Keep breathing through it. Let it build some more."

"It's building..." Chris dug her hand into her stomach as if willing the pleasure to stay in.

"Keep your thighs wide. I know you want to bear down and close them. Fight that urge off."

"Fighting..."

The Mistress pressed the end of the vibrator into Chris's g-spot. That did it. Chris shuddered so hard the stirrups rattled. With a quiet cry, Chris came and came and came. She came so much The Mistress felt warm fluid on her fingers. Finally, Chris jerked back as the orgasm peaked and crested.

Chris laid back on the bed and panted while The Mistress turned all the equipment off and sat it on a towel.

"You okay there?" she asked as Chris laughed tiredly. She looked spent and happy. Perfect.

"I. Am. Awesome."

"You absolutely are."

"And I'm pretty sure I can't feel my legs."

"Hmm...I've never paralyzed someone from giving them a hard orgasm before. This is one for the record books."

"Marry me."

"I can't do that. Not in this state anyway. Civil commitment ceremony instead?"

"I'll send out the invites."

Chris started to roll up, and The Mistress waved her to lay back down. "You might have some brain damage after that orgasm. Just relax until we're sure you haven't suffered any irreversible consequences."

The Mistress soaked a few gauze pads in some saline solution and cleaned the blood and lubricant off Chris. She handed her a pantyliner in case she started bleeding again.

"You can get dressed now. I'm going to clean up and meet you in the other room. Walk slowly. Don't faint."

Chris sat up and looked around, blinking. The Mistress watched Chris dress from the corner of her eye while she washed blood and lube off her hands.

In the bedroom antechamber, Chris leaned against the bedpost and smiled. The Mistress glanced at the clock.

"It's been an hour. Should I let Dad in?" The Mistress asked as she headed for the door.

"Let him in. I might need him to carry me out."

The Mistress opened the door and Kingsley rushed in without a word to her.

"Are you all right?" he asked, giving Chris a once and then twice-over.

"I'm amazing." She collapsed against Kingsley's chest with an exhausted sigh. "I like her so much…"

"What did you do to her?" Kingsley looked at Chris's beaming face with suspicion. The broad, happy smile and relaxed posture was a far cry from the tense, nervous young woman who'd been waiting in this room an hour ago.

"I did exactly what I said I'd do," The Mistress said as she waved at the door. "I gave her my A-game. And my O-Game."

Sadly, that was Chris's only visit to my dungeon. Vanilla people don't come down here very often. And if they do, they never come back. I heard that Chris and Theresa got back together a few weeks later. Where's my medal?

Appended note to Kingsley and not for the files: Speaking of sexy androgynous lesbians…it's none of my business, but you should really call Sam. I know it hurts to talk to her. But I called her after Chris left, and Sam said she misses you too. She also gave me a message for you: "I'm finally getting married, King. You're my best man. Whether you come to the wedding or not, that second sentence is still true."

Tiffany Reisz is the *USA Today* bestselling author of the Romance Writers of America RITA®-winning Original Sinners series.

Her erotic fantasy *The Red* —the first entry in the Godwicks series, self-published under the banner 8th Circle Press—was named an NPR Best Book of the Year and a Goodreads Best Romance of the Month.

Tiffany lives in Kentucky with her husband, author Andrew Shaffer, and two cats. The cats are not writers.

Subscribe to the Tiffany Reisz email newsletter to stay up-to-date with new releases, ebook discounts, and signed books:

www.tiffanyreisz.com/mailing-list

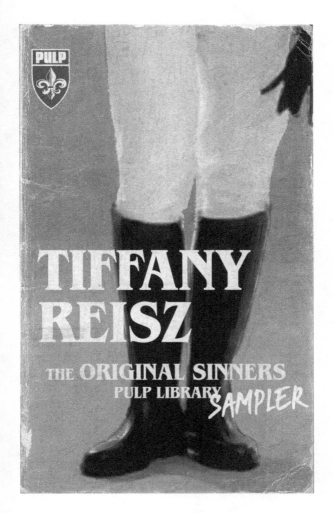

*This **FREE** ebook sampler features excerpts from seven Original Sinners Pulp Library titles. Download at www.tiffanyreisz.com or wherever ebooks are sold.*

SACRED HEART CATHOLIC CHURCH

SINNERS WELCOME